COWBOYS & CUPCAKES

REED RANCH, BOOK ONE

LEANNE DAVIS

This is a work of fiction. Names, characters, places, and incidents are either the product of the author's imagination or are used fictitiously, and any resemblance to actual events, locales, or persons, living or dead, is entirely coincidental.

Cowboys & Cupcakes

COPYRIGHT © 2022 by Leanne Davis

All rights reserved. No part of this book may be used or reproduced in any manner whatsoever without written permission of the author except in the case of brief quotations embodied in critical articles or reviews.

Contact Information: dvsleanne@gmail.com

Print ISBN: 978-1-957233-23-9

The Reed Ranch Series, Book One

Edited by Teri at The Editing Fairy (editingfairy@yahoo.com)

For second chances at life...

CHAPTER 1

"I'M NOT CRAZY. I'M—" Isla Whitlock muttered into the phone before she was cut off by her daughter.

"Are you kidding me? There aren't a thousand people in that place. You're crazy to risk all your money on something that is bound to tank. What were you—"

Isla closed her eyes and pressed her fingers on the bridge of her nose to relieve the growing tension, forcing herself to bite her tongue. Ignoring her rude daughter, she tried to remain in the moment while straining to remember the advice from one of the *many* self-help books she'd surrounded herself with the last three years.

Right. The basic thread they taught was, *her life was her own.* She had every right to do what she wanted with it. The most recent book said to convince herself that no one else's opinions mattered, including her own daughter. Internally, she chanted, *"I'm awesome. I'm the hero of my own story. I'm—"*

Tuning back into the phone conversation for a second, she heard her daughter still ranting at her. She held the phone away from her ear reflexively.

It was so juvenile! Using advice from a self-help guru to try and survive conversations with her own daughter. But still she did it. Concentrating on positive vibes, she hoped to censor the negative predictions that filled her head since hatching this new life-plan and implementing it.

Naturally, she received negativity from most everyone around her, including her ex-husband.

Ex-husband? Why was she even considering him?

Who cared what he thought? Worrying about his opinion was equivalent to relinquishing her newfound power to him. Still, the habits acquired during half a life time were hard to break.

She was free to do anything she chose. She need not consult *anyone*. She could simply do as she liked for once. And she did! She spent her entire half of the money from the divorce on this new life she was building.

The heady experience was completely new for her.

But her daughters had yet to stop lecturing her about it. First, she moved to what her daughters coined, the "middle of fucking nowhere," and then she bought a building.

In that building she now lived and started a brand-new business. *Her business!*

She'd had no such ambitions in her entire sixty years of life! But here she had it now. Being a stay-at-home mother to her three girls, and then even taking on that role again to her grandkids. When her daughters eventually left the nest, she explored several hobbies like golf, baking and knitting, the usual activities people enjoy in retirement.

And then Martin decided he wanted a divorce.

No. Banish those thoughts. No time for grieving over what was. The only thing that matters is now. Today. This moment.

And right now? She was getting scolded by her daughter.

Drying her hands, Isla finished washing out the pans she

used to bake her latest round of cupcakes. Her stomach ached with anxiety, but she ignored it.

All three of her daughters berated her for starting a business so late-in-life. They chided her for allowing an identity crisis to direct her future lifestyle. They kept harping on her that her recent choices were caused by her divorce from their father.

Really? So that was the trigger. Well… duh. As if she didn't know that!

Instead of announcing his retirement, Martin came home from work one day and declared his intention to divorce her. He claimed he was unhappy and no longer loved her anymore, without offering any reason. As far as Isla knew, there was no other woman. He told her she was no longer the woman he wanted to see every day.

Shocked? Traumatized? Humiliated? Heartbroken? Those words failed to describe her reaction. She was devastated. Broken in two. She had nothing left to live for. She was ashamed of herself for realizing what her life had become. She had no sense of value for herself anymore.

Being complacent for decades, when that happened, Isla's response was fast, hard and swift. She replaced her grief with action and decided to change her life by changing herself. She turned to self-help books and decided to make some huge, majestic changes to herself, her circumstances and most of all for *her* future.

Her three girls didn't like her moving on or away.

But Isla refused to remain frozen in time. She made a decision and as uncharacteristic of her as it was, she achieved her goal.

Moving halfway across the state to a rural valley, she found a defunct bakery and bought the entire building that housed it. The two-story brick building had a glass storefront. She liked the downstairs and the large kitchen, as well as the airy, pretty serving area. A stairway at the back led to a single bedroom apartment upstairs. It felt like kismet. Isla sensed it was meant to be.

She became the official owner before breaking the news to her daughters or her friends.

There were no hugs or congratulations, not even the ripple of excitement in response to her revelation. No one endorsed it. They all blamed it on her overreaction to Martin's desire to end their marriage. They all predicted she would soon regret her impulsive act.

Did she ever dream her life would bring her here, in a nothing place like this? No.

But oh, crap. Now, she was fully committed.

She finished scrubbing the pan and prepared to open for her first morning of business. She was damn right about being totally committed.

Her future. She found it. From the moment she saw it, she knew. Something in her gut just knew this was the path for her.

Her new property and business.

She now owned the River's End bakery. It closed two years ago and remained vacant, which was why she bought it so cheap.

After purchasing the building, she remodeled it, creating a new state-of-the-art kitchen and cooking area. She also renovated the small apartment upstairs before moving into it.

She named her new business *Cowboys & Cupcakes*. Frivolous as it was, even to her, she was more than proud to finally have the guts to illuminate her storefront with *Cowboys & Cupcakes* in neon lights.

Cowboys populated the area where she chose to endure her identity crisis. River's End had a distinctly rural vibe with countless orchards, farms, and spacious ranches. Most

COWBOYS & CUPCAKES

of the locals wore cowboy hats, boots, or some other version of what she considered modern western wear. *Cowboys* was the name she selected to entice the numerous small town men she saw everywhere she went. *Cupcakes* advertised her main product. Not just any cupcakes. Hers were fancy, beautiful, unique cupcakes.

Cupcakes.

Who knew they would become her life's passion? Her favorite hobby. And now? It was a new career. An original business. And all because she knew how to make good cupcakes.

Cupcakes were the therapy she used to extract her sad ass from the rut of depression and suicidal thoughts that haunted her after Martin divorced her. She had nothing. She felt like she was less than nothing and never existed. No identity without Martin. No longer Martin's wife. No longer an integral part of a family that she formerly took so much pride in sharing.

Cupcakes were her salvation. At first, she baked them for herself because she craved comfort food but dared not eat a whole cake. Then they became something for her to do to pass the time. They were a constructive distraction that stopped her from crying. She baked cupcakes by the dozens and gave them to her neighbors at random.

After hearing and seeing their responses to her generosity, she wondered, if everyone likes them so much, maybe they'd be willing to buy them? She'd seen their reactions at all the parties she hosted over the years. Most people inquired what new high-end bakery she'd discovered.

Nope. They did not come from any gourmet patisserie. Not at all. They were Isla's artistic exclusive creations.

Cupcakes literally saved her sanity so she naturally named her shop after them.

While Isla embarked on her crazy adventure, her three

daughters continued to withhold their support in any way. All they could do was buzz like irritating gnats in her ear, constantly reiterating what a terrible idea it was. Doomed to fail. Horrendous. *Ridiculous.*

Being called ridiculous was what hurt and humiliated her the most. She hated being viewed as that above all. It was even worse than losing her marriage, along with her sense of self, and the ungrateful family she tirelessly devoted *three decades* of her life to.

Ridiculous way to spend money. Stupid to move so far away. All alone in a dumb, little, hick town. What was she thinking? What was she doing? Those were the topics of several conversations she had with her daughters as she diligently pulled together her business and managed a total relocation. All three of her daughters were exceptional and different, but they didn't hesitate to criticize her decision in chorus, along with their exhaustive disapproval.

Despite her embarrassment and the internal fear she experienced, Isla persevered and finally succeeded. She moved away and opened up a cupcake shop. Her moving day was also disappointing as she was all alone to orchestrate it with the company she hired. Not a single daughter or son-in-law offered their assistance. No one. She realized she had no friends from her previous life. Most of them merely shared her hobbies and some of her time. But no one cared enough to get to know her better.

Isla always thought she lacked any gumption until then. For the first time, she wanted to start her life over in River's End. This one little spot in the world was something she could call her very own and she was more than proud when she selected the name of her new business. Damn it. *She* liked it. No. She *loved* the name she picked. She loved calling it her own too. *Cowboys & Cupcakes.*

Most new ventures took time to draw in enough people

to make a profit. Not a big deal, things would happen eventually and start to turn around…

She hoped so anyway.

She opened her cupcake shop in the middle of nowhere. What if things didn't turn around? What would happen? It wasn't the kind of opportunity she might have in downtown New York City, or even a town with more than a thousand people in it.

She was running entirely on faith. A huge jump with no safety net. A ridiculous leap.

But now she had become really awesome. She was amazing. Screw her daughters for not seeing it.

At that moment, someone entered her shop. The little bell over the door tinkled and she was so wrapped up in trying to ward off any negative feelings that she totally ignored the new sound. Her first potential customer had entered the shop!

"I have to go now, Maggie. I have a cust—"

Her words faded into the abyss and her poor, tired brain could only register *cowboy*. A real live cowboy came into her bakery. With a quick glance around, he zeroed in on the glass case that displayed her prized cupcakes. He examined all the flowered, polka-dotted, striped, and rainbow cupcakes while her heart raced. Thoughts of failing fled like magic from her head. She nearly dropped the phone she was so stunned and thrilled to finally have her first customer.

The cowboy appeared taller when she studied his profile. Gray hair peeked out from the bottom of his black cowboy hat. He bent down with a calm solemnity that one might see from someone viewing a new art display in a fancy museum. He was a large man in both his height and width. He wore a t-shirt with an open flannel over it. The t-shirt revealed toned muscles across the man's broad chest.

Isla's thoughts scattered and almost ran away with her.

Suddenly, Maggie's voice screeched from the phone, "Mom!"

"Sorry, sorry, honey, I really have to go. I have a customer…"

"That's so stupid. *A customer*. What? Is that the only one you've had today?"

Yes. But Isla would rather have bitten her tongue off than admit to that. Why add more fuel to the crazy-mom narrative her daughters persisted in circulating? "No. Of course not."

"*MOM.* Listen to yourself. Seriously, you need to cut your losses now while you still can. I could re-do our room in the basement and let you live there. You could take care of the kids again. I mean… I could really use your help. You were essential to us. Now you're just gone. Don't you miss your grandkids?"

Ouch. Pretty low blow. Isla sighed as the weight of reality and her past of many responsibilities crashed over her like a tsunami. She was impetuous and now she had to pay the price by missing all the daily events in her grandkids' lives. She would try to share their milestones, but her daughter was right, it wasn't the same as being there.

However, Isla needed this more than that. For reasons she could not articulate, she needed this new chapter. To share her house, town, and entire life with someone for three decades only to see it suddenly disintegrate made her reexamine everything she ever believed in. The direction of her life was flipped on its head and she had to adjust and change before she could start a new one.

Her daughters' failure to support her made it easier for Isla to focus on herself for once.

Hell, at least she didn't marry a younger man like their father did. The woman he found was twenty-two years younger than him, and that was apparently no problem for

COWBOYS & CUPCAKES

his daughters to accept. All Isla did was move out and start her own business. That was the tipping point and the trigger that sent them off the rails. Having a stepmother nearly the same age as them was totally normal in their eyes. Strange how adult-aged kids think.

Gnashing her teeth, she still tried to reason with Maggie. Meanwhile, the giant cowboy was scouring the tasty choices displayed before him. Hopefully, he wasn't listening to her side of the conversation. He didn't flinch. Thank God. Lowering her voice, she said, "Of course I miss the kids. Everyday. I miss all of you. But I need something to do all day. Something new and different that I enjoy. I like having a challenge, which is ultimately healthy for my own sense of self, and I'm…"

I want to keep growing. Expanding. At the age when most people retired or considered slowing down, Isla chose to do something new. And much to her astonishment, her choice proved to be elevating, invigorating and exciting. She loved the anticipation and optimism that surged through her when she unlocked her very own business in the morning. She was the owner of the bakery, opening for the day!

Turning on the lights, Isla did a full three-sixty, surveying the small, clean space with a sense of joy she hadn't felt since her daughters were very small. This was very different and very satisfying. She realized the space was entirely of her making. All of it reflected her. Having never enjoyed the control or ownership of anything in her adult life when she was with Martin, since everything they owned was shared, Isla relished this new independence. Martin made all the important decisions regarding any investments or purchases too.

Isla's enterprise would either make or break her. But whatever the outcome, it was all on her.

If only her daughter would say goodbye, she might sell a single cupcake today.

"All you're doing, Mom, is trying to prove to Dad that you don't need him. You can't compete with his new wife. And you're just wasting your money and missing out on seeing your family. You're—"

"I'm done." Done. Isla was thinking that word but it popped out accidentally, interrupting Maggie's rude rant. Maggie's words were hurtful and bitter and she should never have said the things she did to her mother. That's why Isla had enough. She was fed up and refused to listen to it.

"What?" Maggie screeched. The cowboy turned at the sound. Isla glanced at his profile. Oh, damn. Damn. Strong jawline. Chiseled face. Wow…

Focus on the moment.

Maggie.

Isla said, "I'll call you tomorrow. Love you, bye." It came out as a long, sing-song sentence and she smiled when she hung up on her daughter's sputtering response.

Startled that she had the guts to do it made Isla pause for a moment. The cowboy was turned fully towards her and she found herself simply staring at him, not even blinking. She imagined she must look like an owl. His features became a blur as she recalled the courage she had to muster when she actually hung up on her screeching daughter. She was sick and tired of Maggie's bitching so she hung up. Progress at last. Right?

Now she was staring at a stranger. A big, muscled stranger with a strong jawline, hazel eyes and a handsome, but weathered face with laugh lines that brightened it. He probably worked hard, and must have seen a lot of things in his life. His wisdom showed on his face. Isla internally forgot about the stress of her family and a smile came to her lips.

"Hello. Sorry, for making you wait… Um…how can I help

you?" Lord. Her sassy store name didn't match her matronly, unsure tone and stuttering. She feared he would leave before she could manage to take his cupcake order.

"No problem at all."

Oh, the voice... Deep and sultry but quiet and serious. His gaze traveled over her face and then he looked away. He turned, but not in a rude manner, mostly to inspect her sugary confections again. "I assumed you were selling cupcakes, not cowboys, but I've been meaning to check for myself."

Still staring at her cupcakes with intense interest, his deadpan tone kept his words from seeping into her rattled, unsure, insecure thoughts. Her laugh eventually came, but it was a little too late. "Oh, right. The name. I just wanted something... you know, not too... cutesie. I also wanted something that fits in with the area."

He looked up and walked over to her. Nodding, he said. "I get it. I mean you have to name it something."

She smiled. "Plus, I hoped to attract cowboys and cowgirls since they seem to be quite prominent around here."

"True." He flashed a slow-starting, slow-moving grin that grabbed her heart and wrung it out. Her physical reaction made her giddy. She couldn't remember the last time she responded in a physical sense to a man. Not for at least a decade. She felt guilty for not encouraging her own husband more often. Perhaps that was why Martin married someone else.

She stepped towards the cupcake display to inconspicuously dry her suddenly clammy palms on her slacks. She hated her awkwardness. Pulling on the plastic gloves, she stood behind the glass case, clearing her throat before using a casual, professional and totally neutral tone to ask, "What can I get you?"

He stared at the cupcakes some more. Waving a hand at them, he replied, "Do you bake all these?"

"Yes. Every single one. I don't have any employees... *yet*, I'm in the process of looking for somebody." Of course, she was in fact, not looking at all. It was better not to be so honest and open. Instead, she should project success. Fake it until she could make it.

Unless it sunk like an anchor.

Damn it. No. Her damn daughters were the ones responsible for planting any doubts she had.

"How do you manage to get so much detail on such a small surface? These almost look too good to eat."

Bless him. The big cowboy got it. Her cupcakes were little works of art. She even cringed when a particularly interesting or intricate cupcake was eagerly eaten, leaving no more than crumbs that were carelessly tossed in the trash. Her masterpieces were relegated to no more than frosting stains on a napkin. But she dealt with that, seeing how awed people were by them. Their accolades touched her heart and gave her a deep sense of pleasure. Otherwise, she could never have accomplished any of this. The insane idea to move across the state and buy an old bakery at the overripe age of sixty-one began as a whim, then became a dream.

That's why she had to do it.

"If you think they look too good to eat, you must decide if the flavor is as good as they look. My guess is you won't be able to resist eating them."

"Okay. I guess I'll take the black cowboy hat, third one from the left. I mean, yeah, I gotta do it. Double chocolate with walnuts? I can't resist those two together."

"Just one today?"

"Yep. Just one. And a large, black coffee. Good thing my doctor doesn't know about this place." He winked at her. Isla's freaking heart swelled inside her chest.

COWBOYS & CUPCAKES

Feeling flustered by his attention, she tried harder to concentrate. The row of cowboy hat-topped cupcakes were in assorted colors. That was the gimmick. She was glad he took the bait. She slipped the gloves on and carefully lifted his selection, deftly placing it inside one of her custom-made, single-serving boxes. Then, she neatly closed it and carried it to the cash register. "Would you like a to-go cup for the coffee?"

"Oh." He glanced around as if the answer were expected from someone else. "No, thanks I'll, uh, stay here, I guess." He seemed surprise at his own answer. She grabbed an oversized mug, filling it and setting it beside the box before ringing him up and announcing the total. She cringed as she said it. *Was it too much?* He could get the same thing at the gas station except he'd have to settle for packaged cupcakes and reheated coffee at a third of her price.

But the cowboy didn't blink. He just handed her the cash. Waving his hand, he said, "Keep the change."

Tips too.

She kept her unexpected thrill to herself. He might be the only sale she made today. So he was as precious to her as gold. This was the first day she was officially open.

She hadn't approached Cowboys & Cupcakes grand opening right. Mostly because she'd done nothing to make it *grand.*

She opened the store like a phantom. Without any fanfare or official announcement. No balloons to herald the "grand opening" or even flyers to notify the public. Isla was unfamiliar with social media pages and posts. She failed to inform local groups about the shop or having a grand opening. Nope. She simply flipped the new sign on her storefront to "Open" and blithely expected people to pour in.

No one came in but the cowboy.

She wasn't sure how to proceed. Marketing was beyond

the scope of a stay-at-home mother/grandmother with no more than baking in her quiver of skills.

Most likely, social media marketing was the key to success. She had zero idea how to go about it. Her daughters would know, but she couldn't ask her daughters with how disdainful they were of her new life.

So what? She was making her very first sale. And it was all by sheer luck.

The big cowboy chose a seat at one of the small tables. It wasn't by the window as she predicted, but close to the counter. She stared at his profile. She watched him open his small box before blowing on the coffee, and sipping it. He nodded and seemed to approve of it. She tried her best to look busy while peeking over to see his reaction. Hell, he was her first customer after all. The first one in her lifetime. He was her very first transaction. She was officially contributing to the state's economy.

The whole experience was quite exciting.

He unpeeled the paper from the cupcake. Isla's cupcakes were a bit larger than the average ones. To enhance any topping with the effect she sought, she needed all the space she could find. The cowboy took his first bite and chewed it up… Yes. His expression gave it all away. Even the most reticent people, like this man, couldn't conceal how good her cupcakes tasted. Thank goodness. One reaction like that would surely lead to more. Isla doubted he'd leave her shop without spreading the word of his amazing breakfast. He was her only hope of free advertising now.

One out of one was better than none.

He sat there alternately chewing the cupcake and sipping his coffee while staring out the window. She had no idea whom he was but he seemed quite satisfied. The small shop and quiet that descended between them became oddly comfortable. Strange how it seemed that way. It almost felt right. He looked at her every once in a while before turning his head and staring casually out the storefront window again.

Sunlight slowly lit up the sidewalk. It was a lovely view from the bakery shop. Quaint. Small. Cozy. Isla never dreamed she'd be a resident of such a small village. The sidewalk was pleasantly lined with blooming planter boxes. They also hung from the arbor that spanned the length of the sidewalk. The clean, neat, two-lane road only occasionally had traffic and across from it lay a replica sidewalk, more flower planters and a matching arbor. The stores were a variety of sizes and shapes, but all were tidy, clean and brick-lined. Treetops hovered over the neighboring roofs. She looked up at endless, deep blue sky. That sight was in abundance here, another reason she loved it so much.

The cowboy eventually finished his morning pastry and coffee, completely at his leisure. There were no more words spoken between them. Using his napkin to brush the sparse crumbs into his hand, he rose to his feet gracefully and walked over to the garbage can where he deposited his napkin and cupcake box. He carefully set the cup in the tub marked USED DISHES rather quietly. She was mildly surprised at his silence considering his huge physique.

When he turned to leave and got to the door, he glanced around until he found her. Then he nodded his head while touching his hand to his cowboy hat like a country gentleman from an old Western re-run and that made her heart swoon. Her chest swelled. No cowboy ever tipped his hat to her. It was so unexpected and such a sexy gesture. "Thank you, ma'am. That cupcake was delicious." *Ma'am?* Lord, she got so feverish, she could have called it a hot flash but she was long past those. Lord. A cowboy.

Her elated heart pounded and filled her cheeks with

blood as she blushed and replied, "Oh, thank you. I'm glad you enjoyed it. Please come in again."

Nodding with a slow half-smile, the cowboy said, "I try not to make a habit of eating too much sugar for breakfast, but I think I can make an exception for another one of those."

She realized she was holding her breath and needed to exhale. It was all because of his smile. The oxygen seemed to be sucked out of the room. He was engaging, yet almost shy and she found it impossible to catch her breath.

She could not deny her inexplicable attraction to hunky, silver-haired cowboys and nearly begged him to come back that afternoon so she could make two sales.

CHAPTER 2

*A*J REED STOOD ON the incline that allowed him to fully view the land he was surveying. He tilted his hat to keep the sun off his eyes and scanned the horizon. With a grunt, he acknowledged his satisfaction. After all his hard work, this place had truly become transformed.

The moment of positivity was fleeting and a few moments later as he stood there perusing his domain, it vanished. He was proud of his investment. His sweat and persistent effort during the last year was more than gratifying. He single-handedly improved the land that was once neglected, used but never nurtured, and definitely uncultivated for years.

But AJ really wasn't supposed to be doing that. It was *not* part of his plan. The mini-empire he built up over the last two years of widowhood was impressive. But he had to do something after his beloved wife, Kate, died.

He remembered her dying in his arms after wasting away and being tormented by the cancer and treatments that couldn't add any years to her life, only days. They were both retired with plans to travel and explore the rest of the world.

They were also eager to enjoy their grandkids whenever possible and planned to spend the rest of their time together, their "golden years."

But as it turned out, there was nothing golden for them.

Kate died and AJ moved out of the house they built together. He couldn't bear to live on the land they acquired and nurtured and raised their two kids on. He left it all behind, along with the memories that haunted him. For a short while, he lived in his son's large house and tried to figure out what the hell to do with himself.

He received quite a hefty package of funds from Kate's life insurance, but he despised the money. It represented all he had left of Kate's magnificent life.

Because of Kate's life-long high paying salary and investments, added to the life insurance benefits, AJ was now a wealthy man, not only by his standards, but also that of others. He had more money now than he ever imagined. But money could never buy him anything close to happiness. Never.

Losing his wife and being compensated by money proved that point but he already knew it. It did, however, allow him to do something in the time he had left to live. Most of AJ's joy came from seeing his two children, now both enjoying their mid-lives with families of their own.

His grandsons, Ethan and Isaac, were twins that turned eighteen this year. He liked to see them, young men on the cusp of becoming adults. They often vacillated between grown men and little boys. It was entertaining to witness but frustrating for their parents. AJ loved that part of his life.

But the rest of it? The rest of the time he was lonely, merely going through the daily motions of living. Grief and aching accompanied every single minute of his alone time.

So AJ decided to invest his energy and time into renovating old ranches. He purchased the neglected land and ranches, gradually transforming them from top to bottom. He took great pride in that. But his sense of satisfaction was lacking. The old spark of accomplishment that enhanced his life's work was absent now.

He regretted how he resisted Kate's urgency that he retire because his work brought him so much pleasure, self-confidence and pride. It was a major sacrifice for AJ to stop doing it. But Kate was more than all those things to him, so he took her advice and finally retired. The days of being a rancher faded into the past. He slowly warmed to the idea of experiencing new things, as long as Kate was there beside him. Their relationship was what made it all work.

But Kate's confidence and excitement managed to fully convince him it was their next chapter.

After they both retired, however, they never took any of the trips Kate dreamt of. All the time AJ wanted to spend with Kate was ruthlessly stolen away.

Kate got sick and died.

AJ tried, he really did try to pursue their dreams. He traveled but hated every moment of it. He moved out of their house and bought several area ranches. They were in a state of bad repair and dirt cheap. After AJ assessed them, repaired them, and renovated them with love and care, all of which he had in spades, he fell into the role of a land baron.

He undertook the massive job of starting a new corporation. Him. AJ Reed. At the musty old age of sixty-eight, he began a new business that soon turned into a corporation: Reed Ranch Enterprises.

There were several locations now called Reed Ranch. The one he was currently surveying was not unique. The landscape was ideal for the volume of cattle he now ran on it. It was previously owned by a long-time resident of the Rydell River Valley. AJ managed the property before buying it from Tom and his daughter, Kyomi Wade.

AJ was bunking down on the old Wade ranch for the last few months, giving his son, Asher and his wife, Daisy, more privacy at a much more picturesque Reed Ranch location.

Considering the need to identify the five Reed Ranches, they selected names for each location.

Daisy named their place Sugar Hill Ranch after the hill it was built on. Asher spent plenty of time and funds restoring the century-old house to its former elegance and grandeur. It was an undiscovered nugget of unique architecture located deep in the hills, away from any clusters of houses or buildings. The lonely remoteness of this grand, old house didn't bother Asher because the ranch surrounded it.

But the old Wade place AJ commandeered in the last year was about to be managed by another foreman. AJ had someone in mind for the position but had not reached out to him yet. He worked for AJ's brother-in-law, Jack Rydell on the Rydell River Ranch so there was some politicking to do in order to avoid pissing anyone off.

There were three men with whom AJ had worked before and he hoped he could poach them from the Rydell River Ranch to work for Reed Ranches. These three men were solid, loyal workers, with years of employment under AJ at the Rydell River Ranch, where he was foreman until he retired.

Now that AJ owned real estate and a corporation of his own with many operating ranch locations, he could offer advancement and foreman posts to the three men. He felt bad about leaving the Rydells in the lurch and planned to speak to Jack before making any offer to Mack Baker, Justin Kratz and Tyrone Nystrand to work on the three Reed Ranch locations.

Snorting until he all but snickered, AJ tilted his head back to take in the sky above him. "What do you think of that, Kate? Huh? Me poaching labor from your brother? Never imagined a world where that might be the case." He was well aware that no one else was around, and slightly self-conscious to speak aloud.

Did Kate hear him? It was stupid to ask. But he couldn't stop his lifetime habit of discussing everything with her. Her responses came from her past remarks that he held somewhere deep inside him, where Kate was ingrained and remained attached to him.

He didn't expect any answer. The warm sun felt good on his face. Tipping his head down with a long sigh, he started to walk off the small mound he was standing on, when his cell phone chimed. Identifying the caller, he held the phone next to his ear and answered, "Hey, honey."

"Hey, Dad. How's it going?" His daughter was making her daily check-in. Since Kate died, Cami called AJ *every single day*, if she didn't drop by to see him. She and her husband, Charlie Rydell ran a consulting firm that provided investment and financial advice for some rather large and impressive establishments.

For a decade, they lived abroad before coming back to the valley and settling into the Rydell River Ranch. After having their twin boys, now eighteen years old, the family continued to live there.

In her youth, Cami had initiated the collaboration of the Rydell River Ranch with a youth charity called, Shield Shelter, to have foster kids from around the state, travel to the Rydell River Ranch each summer, for a week long summer camp. The entire week was free for the kids. They were able to stay in the Rydell River Resort for their accommodations.

Most years there were two sessions of the camp. The kids were able to ride horses, swim, hike, river raft and other numerous outdoor recreations, that they might not otherwise get to enjoy. When Cami moved over seas all those decades ago, she trusted her friend Brianna Starr to take over her leadership role. Since moving back to the ranch, Cami was once more a pivotal link in the entire organization.

Cami also ran the administrative side of her and Charlie's consultation business, while Charlie handled the consultations. The advances in technology allowed them to live in River's End, which Cami called "the middle of nowhere," and transact with international companies via the computer.

Amazing stuff indeed.

Since her mother's death, Cami felt the need to contact AJ more than he did her. He was aware of that, but didn't let her know he was. Cami's whole foundation belonged to Kate and she'd been struggling for the two years since her mother's death. Cami was a miserable child until she met Kate when she was thirteen. She lived with her biological mother and suffered truly horrific abuse. Social services removed her and she landed on AJ's doorstep at that point. Until then, AJ had no clue he'd even fathered a daughter.

Cami was a gothic, sullen, depressed teenager. A lot had happened to his daughter before he knew about her. He could not undo some of it. Coincidentally, he and Kate had just met as well. Kate formed a strong bond with Cami, which eventually saved the child. At that time in his life, AJ was unprepared for the emotional trauma of his daughter's childhood. But Kate was more than ready. Kate and Cami forged a bond that lasted all of Cami's life.

Now Cami clung to AJ. He knew she was worried that he'd be taken from her next. She disguised her concern by saying she was "checking *on him.*"

But AJ wasn't doing fine either. He liked talking to his kids because they reminded him why he was still here. He found it hard to find purpose in his life and when he did, it strictly came from his love for his family.

Religion touched AJ during the last several decades. He

wanted to believe in something solid after a misspent youth. But the last two years were the greatest test of his faith.

For a long time, AJ was consumed by overwhelming anger. It all felt so unjust and he simply wanted Kate back here, alive with him. His faith failed him at the time he needed it most.

Until her death, he believed his faith helped him deal with hardship, stress, disappointment, and trauma. Only after she died, did he start to understand all those things were doable strictly because Kate was by his side.

He'd been a failure at using his lifelong faith to deal with losing his wife. And that disappointment in himself hammered sharply at his heart.

Nothing was the same without Kate. Even his faith.

Like clockwork, Cami checked on him daily. Sometimes Asher and Daisy called. One of them saw or spoke to him no less than every other day. He was well-loved and well-cared for and hence, they became AJ's reason for getting up every day.

Back to his daughter's current inquiry. *How was he today?*

"Pretty decent. Just surveying Tom Wade's place and marveling how far it's come."

"Dad," she groaned. "It's your place now, not Tom Wade's. He sold it. You bought it. You're the boss." She often lectured him on realizing his authoritative role.

He never had issues addressing a group of ranch hands as their boss. He supervised the roughest men and women that could manage the job duties. Foul language, poor attitude, and violent tendencies didn't faze him in the least. Bring it on. He could handle the work and those types of people in his sleep.

Owning a whole corporation, as well as the land, however, was an unfamiliar and confusing role.

Being boss of a corporation didn't require any physicality

or knowledge of livestock, ranching or farming. It wasn't a role that he could easily step into at will.

His daughter urged him to revel and celebrate it. She claimed, Kate would have been so proud of him for moving on and doing something so grand and important as Reed Ranch Enterprises.

Using the money Kate worked so long and hard to acquire, didn't sit well with him. But at the time, he needed something *to do*. He literally just *had* to find something, *anything* to fill all the hours of the day with.

And fixing up ranches was the fastest project to occupy his time. So using his newly acquired wealth he bought a bunch of ranches and started doing just that, fixing them up.

To his shock? He was making a lot of money.

"Well, it's completely turned around."

"To the point where you don't have to live out there like a hermit all alone?" AJ almost groaned. Cami wanted AJ to live with Asher and Daisy. She preferred knowing he was safely tucked inside their house.

"I'm not a hermit. I see people every single day. I'm living where I work because it makes perfect sense. Plus, Asher and Daisy deserve more privacy together."

"They don't mind you being there."

He withheld his annoyance. Purposely gentling his tone, he said softly, "I mind though, Cami. I still have a mind, you know."

She sniffed on the other end of the line. He cringed for using too sharp of words. He started to apologize when she said, "I'm so sorry, Dad. I didn't mean to treat you like a child and I know you're not in need of care. Since Mom got sick, and every moment after that, you've shown the world that you are indeed fully in control of yourself. I just worry because I love you. But you're strong, and I try hard not to throw my issues at you. Sometimes I'm not strong. I miss Mom so much. All the time."

He squeezed the phone tightly in his hand and shut his eyelids. "Me too, honey. Me too." His throat got tight as his hand gripped the phone. So many tears were shed. Would there ever come a time when their tears simply dried up?

He gulped in some air to calm his grief and thoughts. "You know what, Cami? I have to tell you how much I appreciate you calling me regularly and showing how much you care. You don't even know what it means to me. You make my day. Every day. You, Asher, Daisy, the kids... you're what really keeps me going."

"I'm not so noble. I'm annoying and clingy and I can't get through a single day without hearing my daddy's voice. That's not being selfless, it's just selfish."

He chuckled. "I honestly feel the same way. And I have to tell you, after listening to what I heard this morning, I triply appreciate you."

"How so?"

AJ was eager to shift his aching thoughts about his dead wife and he jumped onto the new innocuous topic. Turning his back to the magnificent view, he started trudging towards his current, temporary lodging. "I stopped into that new bakery in River's End called Cowboys & Cupcakes. I was curious about the name and all. Anyway, I found the most amazing cupcakes there. Each one is a work of art. I hated to bite into it. But the taste? Better than heaven and it fits on a napkin."

"You don't like sugary treats. I never saw you eat many sweets. Never."

He nodded, although she couldn't see him. "True."

"I've always wondered how we could be related when you show almost zero interest in any desserts."

"I don't usually go inside bakeries. The name of it just

struck me. I had to run to the feed store for some supplies on the spur of the moment. I went inside to see the remodel and it has a nice ambiance. You should check it out."

"Well, with a name like that, I'm there. Cupcakes? Hell, yes. But why does that make you appreciate me?"

"The creator of those awesome cupcakes was having a phone conversation with her daughter when I walked in. There was no mistaking that after the woman on the phone line shrieked, *Mother*. Apparently, the cupcake lady's daughter is no fan of the new cupcake business nor her choice to live in River's End. It was appalling how she dared to speak to her own mother. If you'd said what she did, I'd have hung up on you. The poor woman calmly tried to placate the shrieking witch on the other end of the line. But to no avail. Made me so grateful for all the respect and care you and everyone else give me. Even Daisy and the grandkids are always respectful and polite."

"I can't imagine. You'd give me a look that'd shut me right up. Even during my brattiest days, I couldn't handle a disapproving look from you."

"You were an abused kid so it doesn't count. This rude woman has her own kids. So she's at least old enough to be a mother, and not thirteen. She should know better than to do that. The bakery lady stayed calm, considerate, and was even nice to her. She's a skilled artist although it seemed like the daughter had no interest in her career."

"Mom would have kicked my ass if I ever spoke like that."

"True." The image made him chuckle, which felt nice. He liked to remember Kate as they both knew her. Shared memories were more than precious.

"Well, starting a business in River's End with specialty cupcakes, might turn out to be a real challenge."

"That's true. But the River's End bakery was successful for years. It only went under after Greta died and her drunken son drove the business into the ground. There are plenty of customers in this valley to support a bakery. The new place has other kinds of desserts as well. You should go in there sometime. Tell all the Rydells and give her a client base."

Cami snickered. "You're right. And I like the name too so why not? Okay. I'll make sure we go there soon."

Feeling smug as if he performed a random act of kindness, AJ nodded and started towards his truck. He had to unload the items he bought this morning. Still chatting to Cami, he got the latest updates on their business, the boys, and random tidbits that only a parent would care to know. AJ wanted to hear about everything.

Hanging up, he thought about his wife again. Kate thrived on details. When she was dying, she mourned for all the little moments she'd miss. The fussing over a bad day, or describing a stupid client, or buying a new outfit... all the parts of life that came from knowing and loving others.

At least AJ still had his great kids. Not only were they close but as adults, they were also good friends. They *chose* to hang out together from companionship, not because they were blood-related. Having dinner together on random nights, and going over to one of their houses for games, or just hanging out created real connections. Respect. Caring. Love.

After losing his other half, the love of his family was all AJ cared about anymore.

At least they weren't like that shrieking banshee daughter of the cupcake shop's owner. AJ would never claim someone like her as his child.

CHAPTER 3

HE CAME BACK. THE silver-haired cowboy was back in her shop, browsing her shelves once more. Isla was in the kitchen, taking out a fresh batch of cookies. The smell wafted behind her, imbuing the shop with a warm, wonderful aroma. The waves of her hair began falling from the loose tie at her neck. Crap. She was overheated from baking and hadn't so much as glanced in a mirror for hours. She already served three customers so far this morning.

And there was still half a day to go.

Three customers.

That was a huge notch in her belt. Worthy of gloating over.

And the icing on the cupcake was: the cowboy came back for another visit.

"You came back!" she said before she realized she'd spoken the words she was thinking.

He lifted his head in a way that made it appear premeditated. He was so thorough in everything he did. Isla wondered if he ever hurried or spoke loudly. Despite his height and bulk, he seemed to occupy very little space. Only as much as necessary. And he moved like a panther.

Fascinating…

"I sure did. And after my daughter reminded me that I don't like sweets, I decided your cupcakes must be really good."

Her heart pounded in her chest. That smile. Half crooked and so slow to appear. Oh, be still her beating heart, literally.

His words took a moment to register after Isla became so enamored with his smile and his kind, twinkling, hazel eyes. His face looked weathered around his eyes and deeply lined in some places. The deep grooves she saw etched in his face seemed to be the result of a hard-earned, well-lived experience.

"You don't like sweets?" Her eyebrows shot up as his comment finally registered.

Shaking his head, but keeping the smile, he held her gaze. "Not too much. I don't usually crave them in general. But yours are so unique. They're so intricate that I mistakenly expect I'll get a cloying, sugary taste, the kind I can't stand. But no. Your flavors all work together somehow. And I also like your coffee. Definitely first class."

He was right. About all of it. How amazing that he noticed so much from one cupcake.

"Would you like another of the same?"

"Yep. Gotta try the brown cowboy hat today. Looks like plain old vanilla. But I doubt anything could be called plain with your secret recipes."

"You're right about that." Her confidence in her baking abilities was clearly evident, even if it were lacking in every other place in her life. She was a genius with recipes. And cake decorating. Using long-handled tongs, she reached inside the case and selected the cupcake he wanted before taking it out. Setting it in a box near the register, she asked, "Black coffee again?"

"Yes, ma'am, please."

Her mouth couldn't resist smiling.

"What's so funny?" the cowboy asked. There was no hostility in his inquiry, but he wanted to know the source of her smile. Oh, Lord. His use of *ma'am* sounded so unusual to her. She expected such respect from children but not from an adult her own age or older. She didn't fail to notice the twang in the accents of other locals who frequently called her *ma'am*.

"What?" he prompted when she hesitated to reply. He nodded at her and added, "You were smiling to yourself. Either you had an amazing thought or I said something humorous."

"It wasn't anything you said, it's just... I'm not used to seeing cowboys all the time. That seems to be the fashion around here, cowboy hats and cowboy boots with a common twang and homespun gentility."

"Twang? I'm not from this area, so I doubt I have a *twang*." He frowned at her description, looking more puzzled than offended.

"No, it's not a twang, but when people call me *ma'am* I always notice. I never heard it where I lived before."

"Which was... where? The Land of Rude People?" he grinned, softening his words.

"No. In a city far removed from this location."

"And yet, here we both are. Can't be all bad."

She shook her head vehemently. "Oh, no. I don't find it bad at all. It's wonderful. I fell in love with the place the first time I drove down the main highway. I was searching for something with no idea what it was and oddly enough, this place spoke to me."

"You recently moved here?" He tilted his head, then he

shook it. "I did the same thing, only it was nearly thirty-five years ago. Took a job on a ranch and never left. I'd never been here before either. But I was too young and thick-headed to notice the beauty of the area. Glad it spoke to you so loudly. Twang and all."

She glanced away. "Sorry. I'm still learning about country living because it's really quite different. Sometimes, words slip out of my mouth before I can screen them, and I blush and give myself away."

"It's nice to see a face so full of expression; it works for you." He perused her face and the flaming, full-bodied flush that instantly emerged colored her cheeks and throat. He smiled kindly as he nodded, "See? I embarrassed you and it shows."

Dear God, yes. It was too damn long since she tried to flirt with a stranger. She had no clue how to handle it. She was flirting, right? She had to be. But the cowboy was so nonchalant and cool. He said he wasn't married, so he'd probably flirted with a woman sometime sooner than the last thirty years.

Unlike her. She tried to flirt with her husband now and again, but that wasn't the same as flirting with a stranger. Obviously not.

This red-hot, silver-haired cowboy with a slow smile and warm eyes was beyond attractive to her. He claimed not to like sweets but admitted enjoying hers. The best news of all was that he came back. It was the biggest thrill to happen to her in too many years to count.

The churning in her gut accompanied these new and exciting feelings. Butterflies? How many damn years had it been since she felt them? She assumed her sense of feeling anticipation was long dead. Who knew they could still flutter all around her insides? Who knew she'd enjoy those feelings? More shocking? The smile that took over her face. In this moment, in the presence of this man and this interaction, feeling the way she did inside her, she was never more glad to be single.

Blinking when she realized her entire conversation existed only in her head, she knew she'd been silent the entire time.

The juicy, silver-haired cowboy smiled again and said, "Good thoughts?"

"What?"

He nodded at her while collecting his purchase. "Whatever thoughts you were having just now," he replied as he tapped his own face. "They showed. Hope they were as good as you looked."

Then he started towards the front door, using his butt to crack the door open. She nodded vigorously. "Oh, they were. When you get to be my age, you learn to appreciate things more often and differently. That concept just occurred to me."

"Your age?" He scowled. "I can only assume we're the same age. What used to be considered senior years has become middle age nowadays. I fully believe that's where our age lands us." He nodded, grinned and said, "Ma'am."

For distraction, Isla grabbed a rag and started wiping up, busying her nervous hands, while trying her best to look cool and composed. The action made her butterflies go away. Now she missed the damn things. They made her feel giddy, silly, and young. Her interaction with him was pointless but still the main highlight for the day.

"Okay, what age are we are then? The new and fabulous forty? I hardly think so."

"I think so. But I fear my cupcake habit might shorten my life with extra calories."

Fit was a good description for him. How could a man of his advanced years still look like that? Was it the ranching?

Whatever cowboys did, it had to be more physical than all the jobs she knew about at her old home. She still had a lot to learn about her new one.

"Please don't stop eating them. The cupcakes, I mean. How bad could one per day be?" She accompanied her plea with a small smile.

A surprising degree of regret slipped through her to consider him not coming back into her shop. But that wasn't because of losing a sale, it was mainly because she wanted to *see him* again. She hadn't enjoyed anyone so much in decades.

∾

On his fifth visit, he chose a new flavor and design before asking, "What's your name?"

Isla paused from pouring his cup of coffee, now a regular standard with his choice of cupcake. "Isla. Isla Whitlock."

"And is this your shop? Do you own it?"

She did. The pride she felt in confirming that still shocked and thrilled her. Wasn't this sense of accomplishment, purpose and ambition worth the ire of her three daughters? The disdain of her fair weather friends? The pitiable looks she received from the people who thought she was daffy? And now, this giant stranger regarded her strictly as a business owner? Amazing to know how easily she could step into the role she was trying so desperately to fill.

"Yes. I do."

"I'm AJ Reed. I own several ranches in the area. I think my daughter came here yesterday. A woman with short, dark hair?"

"Oh, yes, Cami? She came in with a whole crew." They bought an entire dozen. Isla did not lose money staying open yesterday thanks to that single group. "She's your daughter?

Was her visit owing to you then? Did you suggest she come here?"

He smiled. "I told her how good my cupcake tasted, but I mostly emphasized how unique your creations are."

They truly were. This huge man, who probably knew nothing about gourmet baking and fancy decorating, was impressed enough to mention her bakery to his daughter? His daughter looked about fifty. She was surrounded by several kids and youths. How could this big man have a daughter so old? Was he not so young? "There were a lot of kids with her."

"Yeah, they're not all hers. She lives at the Rydell River Ranch and her boys, the twins, are eighteen. The rest of them were cousins and kids of the ranch workers most likely. It's a busy place. You can always find someone to eat a cupcake with." He smiled and her heart did that crazy squeezing thing again.

"She seemed like a lovely woman."

He beamed with pride and his face and eyes lit up. The solemnity was replaced by a full, shining expression. "She really is. I'm very lucky to have her." He shrugged. "Not to mention my son. His name is Asher. He's a rancher too."

"I hope you'll suggest that he stop by soon." She shocked herself when the words slipped off her tongue like a true salesperson. Who knew she had that hidden talent?

"I will. His wife, Daisy will love this place. Just the setting alone. You know what I mean?"

"The ambiance?"

He snapped his fingers. "Yes, that's it."

"I hope so. I chose this location in River's End to feel homey and quaint. Now, I just pray this small town can provide enough business to sustain me."

He tilted his head in curiosity. "You having trouble already?"

"Well…" Crap. There went her new, awesome salesperson identity. "Not trouble really. No. It's still brand new. So it takes time to let the locals know I'm here…"

"Ahh, heck. That's not a problem. One good word to the Rydells and your shop will be filled to capacity most days. Don't worry. Unlike me, the ranch hands love sugary treats and they also like warm ambiance. Don't worry, Mrs. Whitlock, the cowboys around here will soon be annoying you in spades."

"I highly doubt that. I'm grateful for any advertising. But of course, no expectations."

He turned, pulling his hat down in front as he replied, "I don't try to meet anyone's expectations anymore." Then he had another smile that softened the tone of his words. She stopped and nodded, catching his eye.

He paused. Their eye lock became intense. Finally, she said, "I know what you mean. Maybe it's due to our age? I used to force myself to meet other people's expectations and now… I'm learning not to care what anyone thinks."

"It's a life changing moment when one stops worrying about what others think. You deserve to live your life as you see fit. We've earned that right."

She nodded and his words soothed her like a balm to her soul. She felt like clapping because he spoke the truth. "Exactly what happened to me too."

He held up the coffee mug she handed him. "Remember that, and don't cave to please your daughter."

Startled at his personal words, her mouth opened. "My daughter? How did you—" He knew it was her daughter on the phone the first morning he came into the shop. Isla blushed as she recalled the nasty things her daughter said. "Oh. You heard Maggie. She's been struggling lately with my most recent life choices and other crises in her life. She really isn't like that..." Why was she making excuses for her daughter?

"No doubt. But don't feel obligated to meet *her* expectations. You've got your own life to live. Do what you want to with it."

With a nod, he turned and left. Isla imagined he adored his lovely daughter who seemed so polite, kind, funny and ideal for a customer. Unlike her daughters.

Maggie *could be* those things at times. But not right now and not toward her.

Isla was more than grateful this handsome cowboy corralled a bunch of customers so soon and that his network included the Rydells as well as the people who worked for them. That name was famous here so she had to make sure she impressed any Rydell that came into the shop. The valley, the river and the most exclusive resort in town were named after them. Obviously, they were the stars of this neighborhood.

That was fine with her. She looked forward to tomorrow, when AJ would come back to her shop. The thought of his return instantly perked her up and she suddenly grew anxious for the next day to arrive. She started tidying up but paused, glancing out the window. Sunlight drenched the entire afternoon, making her mood bright and light. The reason belonged to her thoughts about a man.

A customer. A regular that she had to wait until tomorrow to see.

Lord, she felt better than content. She was thrilled. Her thoughts filled her with joy. In no time at all, she felt like a new person. Her decision to find something constructive to fill her time brought her more joy than she ever imagined. She had a new purpose for living. The priceless realization made her smile and she contemplated her outfit to wear the next day.

CHAPTER 4

*H*E CAME AGAIN. AJ the rancher visited Isla's shop daily for several weeks. He ordered every variety of cupcake she concocted and she tried to find new ways to decorate them. Each one tickled his imagination. His appreciation was so sincere, she never could have guessed the large man would be so discerning and sentimental. They started each day now with a brief discussion of the cupcakes and the details of her decoration. He was fascinated when she told him how she wound up baking cupcakes for a living. He listened intently to the various steps in her baking process as if she were a surgeon saving someone's life. Her skills were respectable and noble in his eyes. She could not remember having anyone react to her with such reverence and awe.

AJ was always her first customer of the day. The conversation started after greeting each other with warm smiles and a good morning wish before he chose his cupcake. She explained her inspiration for the treat before ringing his order up and placing it on the counter. AJ paid and stayed connected by bringing up various tangential subjects.

Sometimes he told her about local activities and what to do and see. He often inquired how River's End compared to where she lived before, in Olympia, on the other end of the state of Washington.

Sometimes, he mentioned the names of people who lived in River's End when their discussion turned to gossip. AJ wasn't secretive about himself and loved to tell her about his son, daughter, twin grandsons and all the ranches he owned. He explained what kind of work he did and asked all about her family dynamics. Before departing, AJ always inquired what else she might be doing that day.

She learned the reason why he looked so young to be Cami's father. In his teenaged years, he fathered her without knowing anything about it. The most amazing revelation for Isla was learning he didn't meet his daughter until she was thirteen years old.

The only subjects AJ Reed never discussed was his prior romantic life or inclinations. At one point he mentioned Asher was adopted. She really had no idea if he had a former spouse, or was divorced or widowed or what? Who knew?

For some reason, Isla sensed his former relationships were forbidden to discuss so she never pushed AJ for any more information.

Meanwhile, Isla told him all about her divorce after almost forty long years of marriage, how she dealt with it and why her kids had so much trouble accepting it.

Not only did AJ frequent Isla's bakery, but so did many people with the last name of Rydell. Just as AJ predicted. Family members appeared in all forms: cousins, in-laws, half-siblings, nieces, nephews, and grandparents. Not to mention all the Rydell employees. Isla couldn't remember all of their names.

She met Jack, Ian, Shane and Joey, the original Rydell brothers. Their wives: Erin, Kailynn, Allison and Hailey, respectively. She particularly got along with Hailey Rydell, who was well into her seventies and married to a younger man. The man was closer to Isla's age, but they all three hit it off. Too soon to call them *friends*, but Isla was certainly interested in getting to know them better. She couldn't remember the last time she confided anything to a girlfriend. Those people skills were pretty rusty. But when Hailey kept including her in their conversation, as if she were genuinely interested in Isla, Isla was flattered and grateful.

Feeling like a teenager hoping to join the in-crowd, Isla all but did a jig when Hailey asked her to join her for a walk one morning. Hailey mentioned going down to the River Road for exercise and Isla said she planned to start walking again daily, so presto. Now she was. She met Hailey there and they briskly began their walk.

It didn't take long for Isla to know all kinds of intimate details about the huge Rydell clan, not to mention the Reed clan, as the two were intermeshed.

The Rydells had plenty of kids that were the same age as Isla's.

Cami came back to the bakery often too. Isla welcomed her and was always friendly and engaging. Why? Because of Cami's dad? Was that the reason? No. Well… maybe.

Isla did not see a wedding band on AJ's finger, but some men didn't wear them. Cami never discussed her parents in the plural, but their conversations were not too personal yet.

Weeks after they met, AJ was calmly eating a cupcake when he asked, "You have a chance to get out much? Take a good look around?"

Isla was cleaning up the counter and replacing napkins, creamer and the like, but she stopped when his voice interrupted her. "No, not yet. I've been too busy, just trying to get this bakery going." She waved her hand around Cowboys & Cupcakes.

"You have to take some time off. It's only you working, right?"

Isla shrugged. "As of now, yes. But I think I'll close on Mondays."

"You should hire someone part time at minimum wage to run the shop and give you some time off. Since the cupcakes are already made, can't someone else sell them? If you hire a local, they'll bring in their friends and you'll enjoy the benefits of free advertising solely by word of mouth." She caught the flash of a grin when he asked, "Is it working?"

"Your word of mouth?" Lord. She sounded so flirty. Fluffy. Wispy. Girlish. She feared she'd blush for how suggestive her reply was. Like his mouth was something for her to think about? No. Not at this age. Not after so many empty years. Wait... With him, it might be different. Maybe it would be worth it with him.

"I guess that's a yes?"

Her brain was a bowl of mush. His mouth and other things that she hadn't thought about in decades were flashing in her addled brain. She blinked and all but shook her head to rattle the thoughts out so she could concentrate on what the man before her was saying.

Yes? For what?

Oh, right. He asked if advertising by word of mouth was working. "It is. Faster than I could have hoped." She was gradually making a small profit each day, which was huge progress. Isla was filled to the brim with hope and she all but did backflips at the end of each day when her receipts didn't drag her into the red. Her product was already paying for itself and then some at this point. It wasn't exactly exponentially growing, but also not becoming a loss. She was glad he was the one to whom she owed most of the credit.

"You deserve a commission. But I can't really afford it yet."

His head shook and he replied, "No worries, I don't want it. Wouldn't take it either. No thanks is necessary, not when you earned it. What you've done here is improve the whole street."

"I appreciate your kind words. Thank you, again." Isla was now aching to know if he was married. Her rapidly thumping heart indicated how attached she was becoming to him each morning. What if he belonged to another?

Of course, he *had* to belong to someone else. He was old, like her, and family-oriented. And hot and nice and sweet and kind and handsome. Of course, he was off the market.

But what if he weren't? Impulsively, she blurted out. "Your wife is very lucky."

AJ froze and shook his head. Would he deny it? Or say he was lucky to have her? Of course he would. Most people didn't get to be their age without a spouse somewhere in their history.

But the cowboy replied, "No, ma'am. No wife."

Oh? His abrupt words and cool tone surprised her. No wife or girlfriend? "Husband? Significant other?"

"No one. There's no one significant or otherwise in my life."

"Well, as I've already told you, I'm in the same boat with no one to serve as an apprentice for cupcake baking."

"What time do you close every day? Early afternoon?"

"Yes. Closing time is four o'clock."

"Maybe at dinner time you can start to explore the town a little more."

How could she explain her exhaustion at nine pm? Getting up at four am to bake her treats for the day meant no late nights. All the work and stress she endured were new and wonderfully exhilarating, but they also required brain power. Night for her meant going to sleep.

"I should do that, yes."

"What a lackluster tone. You have no intention of doing it."

She flashed a smile. "You're pretty blunt, aren't you?"

"I don't have time for fake cordiality."

"Right. I get that. I operate from a lifetime habit of people pleasing."

He pursed his lips. "That'll crush your spirit faster than anything. Don't do that. But do take some time to explore the area. It's really pretty. I'll tell you what… I finish at four. How about letting me show you some of my favorite places? We could grab something for dinner? Wanna do it tomorrow night? Or do you prefer Monday afternoon?"

Holy cow. Crap. Wow. The cowboy asked her out!

Her work was done. The awkward flirting was successful. She opened her mouth and closed it again when no words came to her mind. Her nerves gripped every cell in her body.

The idea of going on a date in this lifetime never crossed her mind. Nope. Not once did she even consider it. She was having so much fun talking, flirting and watching AJ Reed, she never imagined the next goal. Yet he just asked her to go out with him. Isla Whitlock, age sixty-one, was about to have her first date in more than forty years. No traditional heroine to a love story could have been more thrilled.

Or was she? Glancing at AJ, she was overwhelmed by his presence and kindness. Damn. And why not? She deserved to be happy and get a thrill every three decades or so, didn't she?

Speechless as she was, she finally nodded before mentally commanding herself to calm down. Trying to sound casual, she said, "Sure. Yes. That sounds good."

"When would you like to?"

"Tonight?" She dared not waste a moment for him to rethink it.

"Sure." He nodded before cleaning up the table and

sweeping off the crumbs into his hand. He always chose the same table and the same seat. She liked knowing she'd become an integral part of his damn routine. She was giddy with pride as she watched him leave and all but kicked her legs high and twirled in circles. Did that just happen? Yes. It did. It really did.

A DATE. Her mind was ready to explode with all the possibilities she imagined. She was more than primed to embrace the unknown and step out of her comfort zone. No more the fearful nobody. The past was over and nothing mattered now but the present. Isla Whitlock was back in the dating pool.

CHAPTER 5

WHAT DID ONE WEAR to explore a rural area and have dinner? A dress seemed ridiculous. Plus, women didn't do that anymore. The formal clothing she wore on her first date several decades ago was no longer the style. She settled for shorts and strappy sandals without heels in case she had to walk long distances. The casual shirt she topped it with looked athletic and casual. Her hair was shoulder length and streaked blond to cover the gray strands. The blond highlights concealed them well.

She tried to remember the ancient pep-talk she gave to Maggie, when she went out on her first date. She told Maggie the guy liked what she looked like and asked her out because of that. Now, however, she found her once sage advice not only hard to believe but also to follow. She felt as anxious as a middle-schooler, but also like an experienced woman who stayed married more than three decades. Odd combination.

The knock on her door came promptly at the time they agreed upon. She valued AJ's punctuality and unwillingness to play games as she flung the door open, ready and rarin' to go.

AJ doffed his brown cowboy hat and his silver hair shone in the sunlight. It almost looked blond in its shimmering rays. His tan enhanced his deeply lined face. Craggy, handsome, but oh-so-interesting. She guessed he was sixty-something. He wore his age quite well and his tough, appealing confidence impressed her.

"Ready to see some pretty country?" he grinned as he looked at her. Her crazy nerves instantly calmed and his smile was so engaging that she soon felt more at ease. No matter what else happened today, she was glad to finally have a real friend.

"Ready to go." She slipped past him and trotted down the stairs of her second story apartment above the bakery. Since when did she become so carefree? She loved living in her own, single apartment for the first time in her life. Isla lived in her parents' house until she was married. Now she occupied a small studio above the bakery in the building *she owned.* Now she was being escorted by a handsome cowboy wearing jeans, cowboy boots and a t-shirt. She never could have imagined any of this happening before.

She liked the new path her life was taking.

"Did you just finish working?"

She followed him by several paces until he stopped in front of a large, brand new, extended cab, white Ford truck. She read *Reed Ranch Enterprises* on the door. "Yes. Please excuse the mess. I came straight from my latest renovation."

He politely opened the door for her. She could have swooned when he held the passenger door and smiled pleasantly. Isla climbed into the colossal beast of a vehicle. She and her ex never owned a truck. Nor an SUV.

But for AJ, a pick-up was simply a logical means of transportation.

"This isn't a mess. Do you still work full time? You're not retired yet?" She didn't mean to laugh but her nerves overtook her. She bit her lip to resist the compulsion to giggle and felt giddy. That was the biggest difference since the last time she dated. Asking her date if he were retired was definitely not a question she'd have asked her date forty years ago. Isla was eighteen when she met her ex.

AJ shut the door and slid into the driver's seat. His long legs stretched out as he flipped the ignition on and switched the powerful beast into gear.

Isla stared at the way the fabric of his jeans strained over his muscular thighs and how the muscles on his forearms flexed. The hairs she saw on his knuckles were also appealing. She decided her level of interest in this man was soaring much too fast so she forced her gaze away from him and looked out the window.

When was the last time she felt like that? She couldn't deny her sexual attraction to him. She wanted to remember every little detail about him as well as this huge event in her life. She never ogled her husband in all the years of her marriage, or felt such chemistry and energy as she did with AJ Reed.

"I tried retirement for a while. Didn't last long. Then I bought a bunch of rundown ranches and became something I never wanted to be."

Startled, her gaze studied his face and she asked, "What would that be?"

"The boss."

"So the Reed Ranch Enterprises is relatively new?"

"Oh, yeah, only a few years old."

"What made you choose to do that?"

"Had no purpose in life anymore. I sucked at relaxation. So I went back to what I knew and took up ranching again. It started when my son asked me to help him buy one, and I was glad to do it. I was more than happy to help him restore it and turn it back into something profitable. I had plenty of knowledge in that kind of thing so I did it. Then another dilapidated ranch came on the market and I snapped it up and started the process all over again."

"You like being a rancher then?"

"Yeah. I was foreman on the Rydell River Ranch for more than thirty years."

"Oh, yeah, the Rydells."

"It's synonymous with River's End. And it's my daughter's married name and my grandkids' last name too."

"You must like being boss if you keep buying up decrepit ranches?"

He sighed as he drove down the twisting, narrow road. "Yes. But it turned out to be quite a disappointment for me. I never dreamed I could be seduced by such a commonplace position."

She liked it when he used the word *seduced*. "I don't think it's anything to be ashamed of when you know so much about what you do. I do the same thing although it's on a far smaller scale. Owning Cowboys & Cupcakes makes me feel like a queen of my own empire. Sink or swim, it's all on me. No one can tell me how to run it. I've never felt so liberated in my entire life. I never dreamed I'd want to be so independent. Or become a real business owner. A small business owner. That label was one I never thought I'd wear."

"I get that for sure. Getting old has given me many labels I never dreamed I'd have either: grandpa, boss, old man… you know what I mean. What other new labels have you acquired?"

"Grandma was the first one I always wanted to be so it came as no surprise. But business owner and boss and divorcee were three I never expected to own. Never thought my path was headed that direction. I always believed my ex and I were exempt from any marital problems. I guess I mistook his silence for contentment instead of contempt. We drifted along for years without any joy or fighting. But I always thought things would go back to the way they were someday." Shaking her head, she sighed. "You don't want to hear about this. It's boring and it sounds so ridiculous now. For the last decade or two, I waited for my spouse to fall in love with me again, without doing anything to make it happen. It was both of our faults."

"It's good to talk about it. Your past brought you here and makes you the new version of yourself that you are now, right? You needed all those years with him to become your true self."

"Is it different for old people like us? I mean, how do we ever manage to catch up when most of our lives are already lived? I find it frustrating sometimes."

"Really? I think it's nice. It's like starting over without any expectations. We've learned enough to ignore the crap we wasted on our youth."

She sighed. "I got married young, so I never really got to waste any crap on my youth. I used to look back and wonder why I was in such a damn hurry? Why didn't I allow myself a few years to misbehave? That's what I regret the most."

"Well, if you were happy, what does it matter?"

"I was happy back then. I can't relax in a haphazard or chaotic setting. Always a planner, I like being responsible and having goals within reach. Safe and sane, that's me; filling the roles of the stay-at-home mom and grandma."

He chuckled as he glanced her way. "By making a move here, all alone, you are anything but safe and sane."

She straightened up. "That's true, isn't it?"

"Yes, it's very true. Not too many people our age would do that. You successfully invented an entirely new identity. And that, Isla Whitlock, takes guts."

Isla was holding her breath and she exhaled slowly. Squeezing her fingers into her palm, she shut her eyes. The pleasure of his analysis was visceral. No one ever noticed that about her. Not even herself.

Yet, she was the only one responsible for this, wasn't she? Despite her pessimistic daughters who warned her not to in the strongest, most unflattering language, no less, Isla went out on a limb and found much more than she ever expected. She recalled her ex's words telling her how stupid she was to invest all of her money into a failed bakery. He repeated more than once that she would get no more money from him, and that was the only money she had. What would she do when her doomed enterprise failed? He wouldn't support her. She was wasting the retirement he spent a lifetime building for them. What a stupid, silly idea to risk it all for one idiotic transaction.

What he said was more or less true. Isla used all of her divorce settlement to begin a business she had no experience with except the creation of the product. She never did any market studies or researched any business plans that people who are familiar with investing might do, because she had no idea how to do any of those things.

"I've never been told by anyone that I had guts."

"Well, thank your lucky stars that you never listened to those souls. Why bother with people who never notice or appreciate your courage?" His tone was spoken with conviction. It seemed to be conveying something beyond the words.

"Are you referring to my conversation with my daughter, Maggie that you overheard?"

"She definitely crossed my mind because from what I gleaned of the conversation, she didn't have any faith in you doing the right thing."

"She's not like that most of the time. She's just worried

right now. Tells me she's going through a lot of stress. The divorce was harder on my kids than it was on me, I suppose. They couldn't accept the idea of me doing something so far out of character. I've become a stranger in their eyes. So what if I exhibit strange behavior? They insist it's an overreaction to the divorce."

"If it were an overreaction, who cares? You're allowed to respond in whatever way you choose."

Huh. Wow. She never allowed herself to step outside the boundaries laid down by her husband and children before. "You're right. I never realized that." Defending her actions without ever owning them was her way of coping. Right or wrong, this was *her path*, and she would follow it as her new direction. "I'm allowed to make as many ill-advised decisions as I wish, because that's my right. They only involve me so why is my family so concerned?"

"Because it never happened before. Age has some damn positive advantages."

"Age? What has age ever brought you?"

"Money for one. The kind of wealth I never imagined. And owning more land than I can see. A wonderful family and fulfilling experiences. And terrible loss. Things I never dreamed would be so hard to endure."

What loss? What was so hard for him to endure? She was dying to know. But AJ turned his head and tightened his jaw so she decided not to ask him about it right now.

They still knew so little of each other and she was content with that, cruising down the country road, letting the sunshine bake everything in a warm glow. It was so vast, it strained her eyes to encompass all the scenery from the mountains to the sky, to the ribbons of river and the dense trees and foliage. Isla felt privileged to enjoy it.

They made idle conversation and Isla asked questions as they passed interesting areas. She felt relaxed and invigorated. It felt good to just be Isla. Who was Isla now? Having never had a relationship without any context or circle of friends to provide something in common, the only thing she and AJ had in common was Cowboys & Cupcakes.

He drove her high up into the hills on roads that were barely accessible: single-laned, deeply rutted, dirt roads. Most were not even paved with gravel. They explored the canyons, the valley and even the mountain tops. Isla found it more than a little exciting. The mountains twisted and snaked all around them, and when they turned or veered off to a side road, she was filled with anticipation. She had no idea where they were and could never have found her way back to Main Street in River's End on her own. AJ drove her to a beautiful, mountain lake with views that went on forever. It was totally different up here. Like another continent.

He parked in the pot-holed parking lot. A few rigs were also parked there. AJ said, "Fishing for lake trout."

She'd heard of trout but never would have tried to find them, much less fish for them, wasting a beautiful evening to do such a thing. Her heart melted when AJ hoisted a cooler from the back of his truck bed. "Brought along some sandwiches and drinks. The sunset's pretty nice up here."

He packed a picnic dinner so they could watch the sunset together in this remote, gorgeous, idyllic location with her? Her heart thumped eagerly and if AJ had looked at her face, the rapture and joy she felt would have been clearly evident. This outing was one of the most thoughtful occasions she could ever remember.

Did she have enough guts to kiss him?

Maybe. But not yet.

Her palms went clammy in anticipation of a kiss. But first, she wanted to enjoy the tasty picnic her date surprised her with.

She followed him down to the beach where the soft, white sand and a park bench awaited them. The lake lapped softly and the water sparkled in green and gold hues in the setting sunlight. Pine trees surrounded by brush peppered the side of the hill and the mountains loomed on their left. She could make out some men rafting in Zodiacs and single pontoon boats. There were a few kayakers to their right. "What a spot," Isla sighed.

"Rat Lake," AJ replied, pausing to set down the ice chest. He chuckled when he caught her horrified look. "Yeah, I know. It's an awful name for a very nice spot. It's different from anything in River's End. With the glaciers up over there and the steep mountains that border the lake. Thought you'd enjoy seeing something new."

She beamed in response. "I'm so glad you did, and I love it here."

"I'm not much of a drinker, so I filled the Thermos with iced tea. Is that okay?" He poured the tea into a plastic cup and handed it to her.

"Fine. Of course, tea is so thirst-quenching. Is drinking a problem for you?"

AJ snorted as he sat beside her. "Yeah… about forty years ago. I quit then and didn't like it after that. Never missed it."

"So it's not a problem for you?"

"No. You?"

"No. I enjoy wine and beer. But nothing much harder than that."

He scooted around until he got more comfortable and cleared his throat. "Well, to be honest, there's more to it. Everyone around here knows all about it. Seems like a lifetime ago…"

"AJ, I don't need to know about something that happened forty or more years ago. I don't care if everyone else knows about it. When and if you want to tell me, I can wait."

He leaned back, resting his arm lightly behind her. "That's refreshing. My entire life history is pretty much part of the public domain around here. But okay. Let's try not telling each other the usual boring facts about ourselves and only say what we want to say—when we're good and ready to say it."

"Or not."

He grinned and her heart pounded inside her ribcage. "Or not. It might feel nice to be a mystery to someone. Decades ago, I was an intensely private person. So long ago, it's hard to remember." He stared at his leg and Isla wondered if he saw something there she failed to see.

"You don't drink or swear either, do you?"

He tipped his head up with a small smile. "Oh, so you noticed that. No, I don't. In my choice of work, swearing is like shop talk. The things I hear could make a truck driver blush."

"Not for you though?"

"No ma'am. No swearin' or drinkin' for me."

"And you're rather soft-spoken also. I noticed that right away. So how do you supervise all the crews that frequent my bakery? I've seen them around town and on the whole, they're very loud, always swearing and often drinking or drunk."

"I demand respect. I'm always fair, there is *no* job I'm above doing, and that I haven't done. But most of all? I know my stuff."

"I like that reason. My husband worked as a manager for a large chain store for decades and he was, in a word, *heavy-handed*. I always found it unattractive. He was so petty. He bristled whenever those below him seemed to know more or questioned him. It made him… appear much smaller to me somehow. He wanted their respect but he never treated them fairly so they withheld it from him. I found him less attractive as he became more set in his ways." She shook her head and then exclaimed, "I've never unloaded like that to anyone. Not to my family or friends and definitely not to my own kids. My ex worked hard and earned us a wonderful lifestyle. I never had to work during our marriage, so I shouldn't complain, I suppose. He was adequate at his job, I guess but not always at his best."

"Like a stereotypical boss?"

"Yes. You could say that."

"You can confide in me. I don't gossip about others." Then he shook his head. "No. You can't know that. But I hope you'll learn that. In many ways with you, it's nice to be so unknown. It makes the old feel new. Is that why you ended up coming to River's End? It was so far removed from your usual choices?"

Flabbergasted, she opened her mouth to answer but closed it and nodded. Collecting her thoughts, she answered, "Maybe. Actually, it might be the real reason why. I've never asked myself, *why here*? Why so far away? Why take a plunge into the unknown instead of remaining in a place that I knew? I think I feared I'd remain the same woman I'd always been if I stayed there."

"After such a major life change, maybe your family needs to realize how much it changed what was normal to you before."

His insight and intuition were mind-blowing. She wished he would explain her odd behavior clearly to her family. He really seemed to get her and so fast, it blew her away. A few casual conversations were all they shared. Incredible.

"You knew I never worked?"

"What do you call raising three kids and making a home for your family? I call it work."

"You're right. I raised my girls to be functioning, decent

women that I'm quite proud of. I did a good job with them, despite what you overheard from my Maggie."

"Then admit that you worked for all those years."

"You know what I mean. I was no manager, holding down a nine-to-five, grinding out a career in a job I hated. I was married at twenty, and once I had my kids I never worked outside of the home again."

"Well, I disagree and think you did. But in the sense you're saying, you're working now. You're choosing to work out of the home now."

"I feel so old-fashioned in this new world and entirely uninteresting."

He gave her a long look. "That's surprising. I find you extremely interesting."

"I can't believe that." Isla blushed and glanced away. "When you asked me on this date, well, to be painfully truthful, I was shocked."

She turned towards him to observe his stillness after her remark. His entire torso flinched. She recoiled with horror when she saw the look on his face. He seemed stunned.

In an instant, she realized her fatal error. Oh, God. She misinterpreted his intentions and said it out loud.

"Date? This? Us?" AJ's tone of voice suddenly became sloppy and inarticulate. Right up until that moment, he was so calming. Now, he literally bounced onto his feet. "Sorry to mislead you, but I—I can't date."

"I assumed it was when you asked…" Isla's previously strong, independent, confident voice faded into wispy brittleness. The unsure Isla returned as fast as that and she was back to her usual state of insecurity.

"It's just… I thought you knew… I mean, *everyone* knows I'm married to Kate. I mean, I just…well, I… am still."

Well.

Isla wondered about the answers he gave her after hearing that name. *Kate.*

Kate was the source of AJ Reed's windfall that gave him a career in real estate before becoming a boss. Kate was obviously dead now. And AJ, the widower, was still very much grieving and hurt. He was merely being nice when he asked Isla, the cupcake wizard, to have a look around the valley. He simply intended to get her out of her shop. No more than that. She was mortified that she allowed herself to see so much more into it than was actually there. Shutting her eyes to the glare of the sun, she also denied herself the beauty of this disgruntled man. She was slightly offended by his shock and adamant insistence that he *could not* date her.

"Everyone who knew her, you mean? Everyone who lives and works in River's End and has done so for years? Decades even? All the time you spent with Kate came before me. I never knew you as Kate's husband. I didn't even know there was a Kate. I know you as a cowboy named AJ who likes my cupcakes. I see only a man close to my age with the good looks, nice manners, and sense of humor that I look forward to everyday. In fact, I can't wait to see you every morning. I don't know you as Kate's husband and I don't want to either."

"But I *am* Kate's husband." AJ shrugged and his tone was strained. He sounded confused. Unsure of himself.

Completely lost.

Again, his stature clashed with his demeanor. His voice was deep but his words were quiet and sad. Shaking his head, he said, "I'm not going to date you, Isla. Not because I don't want to. You're a lovely person, in all ways. I can't date you because Kate's my wife. I consider her my spouse still. I'm a widower, but my heart doesn't know that yet. She's still it for me."

The disappointment Isla felt revealed one thing to her: how much she wished that wasn't the case. She wanted to date AJ Reed. Her age aside, she wanted him just as much as she wanted her ex at age eighteen. This person attracted her. She longed for him to want to be with her. But Kate stood in the way. He was utterly devoted to his dead wife.

"Was her death recent?"

"Recent enough."

"How did she die?"

"Cancer. Late stage before we caught it. She was gone in less than a year."

"I'm very sorry, AJ." Her tone was sincere but her heart ached for him and herself.

He deflated and calmed down enough to sit beside her again. She wouldn't jump on him or try to hog-tie him into dating her.

Although the thought did cross her mind.

"Thanks." He nodded and leaned forward to take her hand. "I'm sorry I gave you the wrong idea. I wish I could date you. But I'm just not... there yet. I don't foresee a time when I'll ever be back in that frame of mind."

"You love her still?"

"Always. She's always been the only woman for me."

Isla hated feeling annoyed by his loyalty. Actually, she envied the way AJ loved his dead wife. She wished he could find more things in his life to love instead of reserving all his love for a dead woman. But the tragic beauty she saw nearly broke her worn heart in half.

Imagine such devotion? It was pretty incredible.

As was the man who experienced it.

"I'm so glad you convinced me to see the area and get out of my shop, which I spend far too many hours in. I was so desperate to draw your interest, that I'm afraid I overreacted."

"You're not desperate."

"Yes. I actually am. After thirty-eight years of marriage. I hate the effect of my divorce on my kids. You heard my daughter. Their lives were turned upside down by something they never thought could happen, and now the family is broken up."

"And you abandoned them by opening your own business and moving across the state all by yourself?"

"I did when you say it like that. I feel like a total wimp around them."

"You're no wimp. Not the Isla I see in front of me." His eyes gleamed. "Kate would have applauded the way you handled it by coming here. She was fierce, independent, bold and brave." His admiration for his deceased wife dripped off him. There was no competition. Isla knew that instantly. No changing this man's commitment and she really didn't want to. Kate Reed was a very lucky woman. So was AJ to find an abiding love that was reciprocated.

"Look, I misunderstood what was happening between us. I accept that. I'm not eighteen anymore and I'm not swayed by my emotions or pride. I'd very much like to be your friend, AJ. A friend is a very precious commodity after a divorce."

AJ nodded as he replied, "I'd like to be friends with you too. I enjoyed having you know me as AJ, not as 'Kate's husband.' Less criticism, and less nosiness. You know?"

"Actually, I do know. That's how people treated me after the divorce. Everyone was different. Nosier and quicker to judge me."

"I'm not sad around you. You have no connection to my life with Kate. So if you can accept my friendship at face value..."

"I can." She smiled with genuine care. Indicating the park bench near them, she sat down and added, "Let's hear about your life, my friend." She smiled as she emphasized *friend*. "When did Kate die?"

He sat down where she indicated and said, "Over two years ago."

"That's pretty fresh."

"Yes. But it seems like forever since I last saw her..."

"Tell me about Kate. I'd like to know all about her."

He sighed, but his tone was contented now. "I'd like to tell you because you didn't know her or us. And I hope you feel the same about discussing your divorce. That sounds weird. I mean, I hope you'll talk to me about it so I can offer you a fresh perspective. I've always been a good listener. Kate did all the talking for us. I wasn't much of a communicator. We worked it out."

She tilted her head and said, "We can support each other as friends with no prior opinions or prejudice because we never knew our spouses."

His eyes gleamed. "Exactly."

"Good." They both settled back and started talking. They talked for hours. The sunset turned the clear water into brilliant colors and the sky faded as the darkness descended and only the stars overhead provided illumination. They talked until it got too cold to stay there. She learned all about Kate and their kids. His greatest sources of pride and frustration. He was quite wealthy now, thanks in part to Kate's good planning. He was eager to discuss all the ranches he now owned. "I'm a land baron," he said in near disgust.

"But you'd rather be Kate's retired husband?"

He stared at her after her precise summation. "Yes. Exactly. Why can't others see that? Everyone tells me how lucky I am to have so much money and land but I find it so far beneath the superior life I could have shared with Kate. Being rich or poor is irrelevant when you're with the one you love the most..."

"With Kate."

"Yes." He glanced away and said, "I'm sorry. Too much information about Kate?"

"No. You heard my long tale and bitter divorce."

"I like getting to know you."

"Well, knowing you is knowing all about Kate too."

He slipped his hand over hers. They quietly held hands while staring at the darkness. It wasn't anything sexual or flirtatious. It was appropriate for a friend. "This was nice tonight. And I thank you."

"My sentiments exactly, AJ. I truly got to know someone tonight, and it's been a very long time, maybe decades since I've done that or even made a friend. A true friend, that is." She let out a laugh. "I hoped we were having a date. But it turns out this was better than that."

Oh, the irony. Describing her prior life and what happened to her was good therapy and it purged the toxic feelings she had no idea she still bore. AJ was the friend she needed. One who wanted to hear all about her. Not her previous life or her ex-husband or even her kids. Just her.

"I feel almost selfish to have you hear my side regardless if I'm right. You don't know my ex or his side."

"Same here. You don't know if I'm perceiving it correctly either. Different circumstances, but the same result. I had no idea how good it feels to share our most intimate topics with."

Their hands squeezing, they sat in silence for a long time. It was the most profound way of bonding for Isla. She couldn't compare it to anything in her past.

Their clasped hands connected them beyond their age or life crises, and they were simply two human beings together.

Two kindred spirits.

Two friends.

Two wonderful friends.

There was one sentence that he kept repeating to her,

"Kate is gone. I know that. I really do. But oddly enough, no matter how often I remember that, I can still fall in love with her every day."

Well. What could Isla possibly say to equal or surpass that kind of love and commitment? There was nothing she knew to compare with it. The biggest thing she learned that night was her friend, AJ might be the most loyal person she ever met.

CHAPTER 6

*T*HERE WAS A LOT for AJ to think about. Lying on his narrow bed at the old Wade homestead, his mind was centered on his *new friend*, Isla. He was glad she simply didn't walk away from him, and believed it spoke well of her character. He overreacted to her misconception that they were on a date, and all but humiliated her. His unscreened horror could have been enough to make many women instantly abandon him. Or at least, defiantly cross their arms, turn away and demand that he take them home. He couldn't blame her. Isla was just as embarrassed as he was, but she quickly adapted to the new circumstances. He could only admire her quick thinking. It was a microcosm of her achievement in moving across the state from her kids, her grandkids and the only life she knew to open Cowboys & Cupcakes.

AJ found Isla interesting in many ways. He guessed she was in her late fifties or early sixties. He liked her warm brownish-blond hair with brighter highlights that reflected the sunlight. She was short, but well- endowed, with rounded hips and a full butt. She had a pleasant face and an unsure smile that was fun to coax from her.

Isla was practically the antithesis of Kate. Kate always wore her hair in short, blond locks, standing tall and thin, always so bold, brash, intelligent, funny, kind-hearted, and a source of endlessly loyal love. Kate's image stayed in AJ's mind.

Isla left her whole family behind. AJ bore no judgment, but that was the truth. It was a bold and pretty shocking revelation. AJ's only reason for living now was for his family.

He couldn't forget the screeching voice of Isla's daughter on the phone. Isla certainly defended her and insisted she wasn't really like that. Well, he begged to differ.

Anyway, the cupcake lady actually surprised him when he got to know her better. Apparently, a date with him was desired even after her harrowing divorce.

Her words echoed in his head over the next few days. Her story. Her side of things. Subjective tales are always skewed, aren't they? But when he looked into her eyes, he saw the truth. She was overly self-deprecating and way too critical whenever she described herself. Being on her own and displaying confidence seemed to definitely be a new way of life for her.

Cupcake lady was unhappily married for years. A decade? Two decades? Maybe she only married him to avoid being alone. Martin. From what she said, he seemed very uptight and downright cheap. That was AJ's conclusion, not hers. Isla was surprisingly kind when she spoke about him. AJ welcomed her description of him without reproach or judgment.

Just before Martin Whitlock retired he asked Isla for a divorce. Didn't seem like he had anyone else waiting in the wings. He just stopped loving her. The abrupt change of lifestyle and lack of identity were Isla's main problems, in AJ's summation.

Isla was all alone for the first time in her life. She feared anything that sought to solve her loneliness. He completely emphasized with her perception. "I felt the same way for the first year after Kate died."

"Being in a room of people was when I felt most alone and detached from humanity."

AJ stretched his legs out and simply said softly, "Yep."

Exchanging looks, he realized how intimately she felt his pain. More than anyone else did.

That common understanding was what stuck in AJ's head the most after he dropped Isla off and returned to the empty, old Wade Ranch.

∼

"WHAT'S UP?" Jack's voice interrupted AJ's thoughts. He was standing against the fence, staring into the horse pasture. It used to be the main arena until it burned down in the fire several decades ago. Things were later rebuilt. But in that moment, AJ was lost in another time. He was watching Kate in the arena when she came there for riding lessons and AJ was assigned to teach her. Before he knew her, slept with her, or ever dreamed of spending his life with her. Despite being from the city, AJ never expected to fall in love with her, although he desired her at once.

Kate scared and intimidated him. She initiated everything. First talks. First jokes. First conversation. First kiss. First sex. First date. First love. Yeah, most of his life wouldn't have happened without Kate starting it.

Jack Rydell was Kate's half-brother and the man who interrupted AJ's musings. Shaking it off and turning to his lifelong friend and brother-in-law, AJ replied, "Just remembering…"

"Ah…" Jack came beside him and stared out at the green pasture. "This place has a lot of goddamned ghosts for us old timers, huh?"

"Too many now."

"That why you prefer to stay so far away?"

He sighed. "Yeah. It's hard for me to come back here. Sorry I don't visit much."

"Nah. Don't be. It's hard enough to live without her. Do whatever you need to. You know that, AJ."

"She left me money to burn."

Jack snorted. "Not a bad thing to most people."

"It's the worst part of it, besides missing her."

"What about the ranches? You own… what? Five now?"

"Eh. More like four. The fifth one is Asher's."

"Well, at least you still have a purpose."

"I do. Look, you can say no, but I prefer an honest reply. Don't pity me because of Kate. Okay? This has nothing to do with losing Kate."

Jack nodded. "Okay. Fine. You got it."

"I want to ask Justin, Tyrone and Mack to fill the foreman positions on my ranches. They're the best guys here, so I know it's a hardship on you. But your foremen jobs belong to Pedro and Jordan. The other three can't get higher promotions here. My offer would give them that. I can't manage all the land by myself. I need good guys that I can trust. So I'm asking to poach them from you guys."

Jack snorted. "You trained them, AJ. Of course, you should offer them any job advancements. They're all worthy. Pedro will be pissy about it, but you can handle him… right?" Jack wavered a little as he side-eyed AJ, who chuckled. Pedro was a fierce foreman. Excellence was his only standard. Pedro was the benchmark, and he took care of everything with preciseness and efficacy. "On second thought, that's my only stipulation. You have to tell Pedro."

AJ let out a snort. "I'll tell your fierce foreman. I really wanted him, you know. But I knew he'd never leave you to work for me, and you'd kill me if he did."

"Damn right. I'd have done the same if anyone tried to take you from here."

"Except for Kate." He smiled while remembering all the discussions they had about retiring so they could travel and watch the grandchildren. AJ resisted, but finally conceded with a bit of regret. He loved working at the Rydell River Ranch. He treasured the hours he spent with Jack, Ian, Caleb, Asher, Jordan, Pedro, Joey, and the list went on.

"Just Kate," Jack agreed. Their gazes stayed pinned on the horses grazing a few yards beyond them.

"How're the boys?" Jack asked after a long silence.

They shared twin grandsons in Ethan and Issac. So many tangles, but in the end, a blessing.

"Still struggling. They come to see me a lot. I think it's just an excuse to check up on me."

"Yeah. They worry a lot about you."

"Nothing to worry about. I'm still here and kicking. Just sad while doing it."

"AJ—"

He blinked at Jack's tone. "Don't, Jack. I know. I know how much you miss her too."

"Not like you do."

AJ tried to swallow the lump in his throat. "No. No one will ever miss her like I do."

After a long silence, Jack cleared his throat. "Oh, by the way, I met your friend."

"Friend? What friend?"

"That bakery lady with the cupcakes. I don't remember her name. Everyone said you recommended her cupcakes and since you don't like most desserts, I had to see for myself. So I went there to try them. Those treats are evil-good. She seems awfully nice too."

AJ's gaze stayed on Jack who tried to be nonchalant but couldn't convince AJ that he hadn't rehearsed his comment. "Why did you call her my friend?"

"I saw you together. At the lake the other day? I was fishing with Ian."

"Oh."

Silence fell again. Clearing his throat, Jack said in a very soft voice, "Kate would want you to find new friends."

AJ stiffened and glared straight ahead. "Don't."

"I know." Jack stopped and lifted a hand which he set on AJ's shoulder. Squeezing it, he said, "But believe it. No one else will say it to you. It's okay to…"

"It's not okay. I can't. End of story."

"I get it. Really. I do. More than you know. I said the same thing." He started to walk away but turned back to add, "Until I met Erin."

AJ damn well knew that Jack lost his first wife and met Erin seven years later, whom he married and had another child with. But AJ wasn't like Jack. It wasn't the same thing.

Oh, well, at least he got the three foremen without pissing Jack off. So mission accomplished on that front. Now he had to deal with Pedro. Pedro would be pissed, and he was annoyed Jack insisted he tell Pedro.

Decades ago, Pedro was an eighteen-year-old kid that AJ hired. Now, he ranked as someone that AJ respected and didn't like to upset. He was better than excellent at running the ranch with so much attention to detail, he was even better than AJ.

As for Jack and his unsolicited advice, well, hell. Who asked him? Damn the small towns where everyone knows everything about everybody. Maybe he should do what Isla did. Maybe he should sell the ranches and move to the city where no one could give him any lip about having a new friend.

AJ really had fun with Isla and refused to let idle gossip stop him from seeing someone who was a good listener. She was proud to be *his* friend. End of story. Isla marked a new phase in his grief and he was ready to enter it. He deserved to have a confidant and idle gossip couldn't taint that.

∼

AJ IGNORED anyone who asked him about his friendship with Isla. He would not allow anything to threaten what turned out to be the best antidote for his grief since Kate died.

He made a daily ritual of visiting Cowboys & Cupcakes and started every day now with a cupcake. He liked having somewhere to go where another person counted on him showing up. That meant a lot to him. Until he met Isla, AJ was prone to staying in bed, doing nothing, allowing the weight of his grief to prevent him from getting up. Sometimes, he couldn't even brush his teeth.

There were days that seemed so pointless that any ambition he had in mind evaporated.

But Isla asked how he was each morning and he found himself looking forward to their exchanges. That was his reason for waking up. He liked having someplace to go.

He ate Isla's cupcakes and drank her coffee. On some mornings, they talked more than an hour. When she had a rush of customers, AJ marveled how far her business had come. He glowed with smug satisfaction when her shop was crowded and thriving. On those days, however, she was too busy to talk so they only exchanged a few words.

Seeing Isla, no matter if it were for a few moments, or a full hour, kick-started *all* of AJ's days now.

They went to dinner sometimes and AJ showed her other places he liked in the valley. He took her to a local rodeo, because she never attended one before. AJ toured the rodeo circuit for years so hearing that was impossible for him to imagine. He had fun introducing her to his favorite pastimes and places.

Learning about each other's backgrounds was also fun and kept their times together from ever becoming boring or ordinary. He appreciated her sense of humor and swift comebacks and often enjoyed sparring with her. Kate and he had similar interactions.

So AJ finally had a friend that changed his life. That really meant something to him. His days weren't so black. Dark gray still, but not black. Isla glowed like a pinprick of light in a blackened, burnt out world. Isla gave him moments to appreciate and AJ often thanked her.

The problem with her friendship was that he started to think about her when he wasn't with her. He started to save up little tidbits of his day to tell her about, over their morning cupcake. If he thought of something funny or interesting she might enjoy, he text it to her. She always responded and those texts made him smile, as his entire mood seemed to get better after hearing from her.

In short? Their friendship became one of the most important part of his days and her smile the thing that started to fill his lonely, dull, often bored heart. His sad heart. His broken heart.

For the fist time since Kate died, some days started to seem not so endless, pointless and terrible.

Because no matter how bad the night was, each morning there would be Isla.

CHAPTER 7

CREAK. THUMP. CREAK. THUMP. Creak. Thump.

AJ listened to the noise as the wind gusted before the door banged again. The barn door had big, rusted-out hinges that were no defense from the night winds that continuously blew the door open and shut with methodical bangs. Tossing onto his left side, he covered his head with the pillow, but the creaking and subsequent thump as the door swung against the side of the barn, prevented him from getting any sleep. He wrapped the pillow around his head to suffocate the noise to no avail.

The wind had an erratic pattern but the *creak... thump* persisted. Now it was slightly muffled but definitely still there.

AJ stared out from his bed, watching the yard light make shadows in the room. There was enough light to see the clock and the hands ticked off the seconds. They passed by so slowly. Could time move any slower than in the middle of the night, two o'clock to be precise, when everyone else is sound asleep?

But sleep refused to come tonight. AJ flopped over onto

his back. Staring at the flickering circles and shapes created by the outside light, he could only listen. The clock was soundless, but the persistent creak and thump made him think of an old-fashioned clock ticking away. Tick tock, life was slowly melting away. Second by second. Lying there, alone and staring at the ceiling, he fully felt his life ticking away. He squeezed his eyes shut but that only made him think and hear more. He flopped over again and started the same exercise, hoping it would finally work. In his mind, he tried to ignore the things that kept him up so often by imagining them dropping out of an airplane into oblivion.

The pain. The sadness. The loss. There were so many things he wanted to tell Kate today. Trivial details and random thoughts, facts about their kids and the opinions of their neighbors. Life in all of its mundane details. Kate was missing that now and AJ missed living with her.

There was no one to tell those things to anymore. Not a soul. Not the small stuff. The banal stuff. That was reserved for your spouse. The only person who cared about all the nitty-gritty particulars that made up the moments, hours, days, and weeks spent together.

Instead, AJ ached in his heart, like he was being stabbed in the chest. It happened so often that he was getting used to it. It had simply become part of his existence. No one to talk to. Nobody to embrace and cuddle and just breathe together, feeling grateful not to be alone. The nights were much longer and sleepless, but mostly, lonely. Being awake when everyone else was asleep happens to everyone. But that sense of loneliness that never left AJ made it even more bitter.

AJ was all alone now and forever.

He opened his eyes and stared up at the ceiling as the wind howled. That ceaseless rhythm. The longer he lay there, the more alert he became. The wind also grew louder. Growling in annoyance, he flung back the covers, turned over, and got out of bed. Pulling his pants on, he tugged a hoodie over his shoulders and stumbled into his boots before flinging the front door open.

The squeaky barn door had to go or else he was. Gritting his teeth, he rushed into the shop and searched for the tools he wanted. Taking the hammer, he started pounding it against the bottom end of the lowest hinge. The hinges were old and the wood splintered as he pounded harder and harder. But the thrill of splintering the wood and releasing his stress in such a powerful way filled him with strength and a sense of control. Many times in succession, he slammed and pulled on the hinges, but they refused to budge.

It would have been much simpler if he had another person to serve as an anchor and hold the door still. It swung forcibly in the wind unless he held onto it, which prevented him from undoing the hinges.

In no time at all, sweat slickened his body and rolled down his forehead, but he hammered and clawed at the hinges again and again. When the wood ultimately surrendered, it snapped and splintered before finally letting go. The first hinge finally came off. The door frame was damaged beyond repair. One down, two to go.

When the top hinge was all that held the door on, it was so bent and crooked, it looked like a tooth clinging only by the thread of a root. With the smallest tug, out it came. That was after he pulled and tore everything around it. The weight alone would have killed him if he fell under it, but he was careful to heave it away from his body.

Success.

He did it! No more creak and thump. It. Was. Done.

He stared for a few moments at the gaping hole he opened. It was quiet now in the yard as his sweat dried and he started to cool down. His breath became regular too.

Eventually, he realized that he just destroyed his own

property for a stupid reason. He impulsively ripped off a perfectly fine, working barn door because the wind was making it thump all night and the old hinges creaked. Really? A few shots of WD-40 would have been a much more reasonable solution. A blush warmed his cheeks as he realized the absurdity of what he'd just done. The hammer was still in his hand and he looked at it vacantly.

Perhaps he wasn't all there anymore.

He was so tired of feeling lonely. So goddamned tired of not having someone there. Nothing else to say except he wasn't in pain or sad. He was just lonely. He hated that feeling more than any other he could remember.

This stupid episode merely added more work to his endless chores around the place. This did not need to happen.

But his loneliness wasn't something he could share with anyone in his family. He was the sole recipient. In the middle of the night... that was always the hour when he missed Kate the most.

Rubbing his eyes, he set the hammer down. He was so tired. So exhausted from feeling that way.

Turning around, he went back to the house. It was silent now. No creak. No thump. No Kate.

And this was *not* the house he shared with Kate. So why did it feel like she was missing? Sighing, he knew why, 'wherever they were together' was home. The house never mattered.

He grabbed his keys. Where would he go? What would he do?

For the first time since his wild youth, he felt reckless and impetuous. He had to end this gnawing loneliness and the angry, almost violent feelings it evoked.

Starting his truck, he roared out of the old Wade place, and drove down the dark road. Deserted at this time of night, he drove without any direction in mind. For once, it was more important that he stop feeling this way than whatever impression he might make to an onlooker.

He parked across the street from the little bakery where he spent most of his time lately. He liked to come here because things didn't seem as dark or hard or lonely. The moments spent with the kind, nice, sparkling cupcake maker stirred up feelings that were fresh and different.

Not family-oriented.

He pocketed his keys as he crossed the road and contemplated the front of the pretty storefront. Well, hell. What could he do this late at night? He had no plans to break the door down as he did his own. Knocking on the front door would no doubt scare the crap out of the woman sleeping upstairs.

His rational thoughts were sleeping even if he weren't.

He went around the back side of the building where the door to the overhead apartment was located. He feared he would scare her. No, *terrify* her.

Yet he still climbed the stairs. He stared at the building. The lights overhead made him blink. Did he dare?

Apparently, yes. He knocked.

After a few moments, he heard movement so he called through the closed door. "It's only me, AJ."

The pace of the steps increased. The door cracked open and Isla's face peeked out, just her profile until she could confirm his identity. Then she leaned back and opened the door wider. "AJ? What happened?"

Crap. He scared her and now he was worrying her. Her mouth grimaced with anxiety.

"Oh nothing. I just couldn't—" *Sleep.* The word remained in his mouth. It felt like an old wad of gum. He shouldn't have come here. Reality dropped on him like an anchor. He was a grown-assed man. No, he was an *old* man. Well past mid-life crises and any other stupid impetuous pursuits. But there he stood, wishing he could disappear.

At least his loneliness was gone. Now he felt like a foolish jerk.

"I'm sorry. I was in a reckless mood. I shouldn't have woken you..."

He all but rushed to flee when she stepped out and stopped him with her hand. "Well, you have now so come inside and tell me why."

Startled by her command, he looked at her more keenly. She was quite short, something he wasn't used to. Kate could nearly look him in the eye on her bare feet.

But Isla wasn't Kate.

And he specifically came there to see Isla. Her gaze swept over him. What did she see? How haphazardly he put on his clothes? Sweat-dried hair? Who knew? She pursed her lips and indicated for him to come inside. Feeling contrite, AJ complied. After she shut the door, she turned to him.

"Bad night? Things become too much?"

Startled at her prescience, he nodded. "Well... yes. How did you now?"

She snickered. "I was divorced by a man I'd spent almost forty years sleeping beside. I know a thing or two about bad nights. Your thoughts are much louder when there's nothing to distract you from them. The darkness becomes so vast. Time is irrelevant. The clock keeps ticking."

"Like your life is ticking by and you wonder whether losing it is the worst thing and you wish it would just go faster?"

"Yes. It feels like an elephant is sitting on your chest and your damn rib cage can't support the weight and you just wish it would break and collapse. Is that the feeling you mean?"

He tilted his head. "That's the one. What... what do you

do when that happens?"

She sighed. "Nothing works consistently. Lie there a little longer. Cry. Or get up and pretend to do something productive."

"I pounded the door off my own barn."

"Oh? Huh. Because…?"

"The wind kept making it swing and it creaked and thumped against the barn. I thought it was keeping me up. After I busted it off I just stared at it on the ground and still…"

"You wondered, 'why should I do all this if I'm alone'?"

"Yes." He was relieved to hear her words. The common perception. Their gazes locked and the mutual understanding they felt was deep and instantaneous. His previous loneliness hadn't fully retreated, but it was definitely pushed back. Maybe he could survive this.

"I feel so confused sometimes. I don't want to be gone from here. But then again… it's just so hard to be here too. Sometimes."

"Yes. I know the feeling."

He nodded and cleared his throat. "I didn't know anyone else felt that way."

"I think everyone feels that way especially when they endure a crisis of some sort."

"Right. I guess I was lucky that I never knew about it before. Did you sense it was coming? Before it happened?"

"My divorce? Yes. I knew it when he lay right next to me. Right there. His body was warming mine until it wasn't and the coldness of being all alone was detectable even then."

The idea of that struck him as hard to handle. How could he lie beside Kate and not love her? That would have been sheer torture for AJ. He had Kate's love. Real, deep, abiding love. Did Isla ever have that?

"Was there ever a time you didn't feel that way?"

She looked away. "I think maybe when we were younger, but the more recent years are much fresher and I don't remember the older ones as clearly now. I just recall the ending years, when my chest hurt often. And hard. And yet, I didn't want the divorce."

"Because you were so used to him? And your lifestyle?"

"And because of our family. I had a vision of myself and my life. This…" She waved a hand around the room. "This was never, not even for a moment, the vision I had of me in my sixties. Never say never. That was the real lesson." Her head tilted. "Is it worse to lie beside someone and feel alone and lost, or be truly alone without anyone to make you feel those things?"

"Both sound equally bad."

The corners of her lips barely curved upwards. "They are bad."

"I feel bad. Tonight."

"Did you come here because you wanted me to commiserate with you or make you feel better?"

Unsure, he pondered her question in earnest. Finally, he said with confidence, "Because I hoped you'd make me feel better."

She nodded. "Okay, then."

"What does that mean?"

"That means you said the answer I preferred."

"Which means what?"

"Come with me. To bed."

The sharp, clear statement startled him. To bed? Them? Here? To bed? For what? Sex? Did he come here for that? Most people would assume that's what he wanted after knocking on her door at three in the morning. But did he have that thought in mind? He was seriously unsure of his own intentions and heat filled his cheeks as words fled his mouth.

Isla gave him a glare. "AJ, you came here for a reason and I doubt you wanted a cupcake at three in the morning. Man up. Admit it."

"But... I... we... should talk. Figure out things. Let me explain, at least. I mean, I said I could not date. I feel married to Kate still. I'm Kate's husband. Maybe Kate is the reason I'm here. I don't want to be the one who hurts you. I don't want to make my problems yours. Yet—"

"Yet here you are. With me. Right now. I don't ask for love or promises. I don't want those. I spent most of my life married. Understand this now, I don't want to be married again. The last two decades I was married but I was all alone. The only thing I've done that was impetuous, crazy and risky was to move here, by myself, and open this business. I love living by myself. I'm sorry you feel lonely, because I feel like a wild animal getting released. I've been set free for the first time in my life. It's finally my own life. I own it now. All of it.

"I can let a big, husky man like you into my apartment at three in the morning, because I choose to do it. I never did that before. So if you think I'm looking for what you and Kate shared, I'm not. You said you came here because of me. That's it, that's enough for me. It's all I want from you, in fact. You wanted me. *Right now.* I'm the one you needed and I'm good with that. I'm still free and wild and able to do things in the moment because *I can.* Maybe just for fun. There's a carefree sense of abandon that I never got to enjoy before. All my decisions were centered on kids, grandkids and a husband who didn't deserve my fidelity, loyalty and faith.

"But you, AJ? I'm not offering that to you. I want us to have fun. I want us to be present in the moment. I want to help you get through a bad night. I'm happy to offer you that because it can't hurt or break me."

He blushed and felt bad for assuming all matches should

be what he had with Kate. Fidgeting now with his nerves for being so presumptuous in thinking he had any power to hurt Isla, he didn't know how to respond. Finally, he threw up his hands. "I haven't dated in three decades either. Kate did all the date-planning. I don't really know how to do this at all."

She smiled softly with gentle understanding. "I used to think like you. I promise that when you let it go, you will get a taste of freedom. It's not life or death. No blood oath. It can be sex. Or friendship. Or a hug. Or all three. But it's okay because, after all, you're still alive."

He sighed heavily. "I thought I didn't need anyone but her. Her memories were enough to sustain me to my death. I would be—"

"Her husband for the rest of your life and that would be fine with you. Maybe at three o'clock in the afternoon it's fine. You're busy at work, making physical repairs to your many ranches and the kids and grandkids are always available. But not at nighttime. At three in the morning, it's not fine anymore."

"Yes. It was overwhelming. And it just isn't enough." AJ was racked with shame for assuming he was long past any physical needs, wants, and desires. They all died with his wife. For a time, they did perish. Now, he couldn't suppress that urge so easily and it surprised him.

"So we're friends. We might hug and have sex. I'm a free adult and so are you. One or both or neither of us could get hurt. Or become more invested than the other. But hell, AJ, I lived an uneventful life without truly engaging because I always feared what might be. I don't want to hesitate anymore."

"I don't think I want to either."

"Then… Don't. Come to bed. With me."

CHAPTER 8

LEADING AJ BY THE hand down the hallway, Isla's entire body zinged with newfound energy. He was so big, he filled the space behind her and seemed to create a wake after him. His presence loomed in the most enticing, exciting way. Her nerves were ragged but no match for the joy that was filling her.

AJ came to her.

Oh, hell. Did she really mean the crap she spewed about just being friends with this man?

No. No, of course not. She wanted AJ in a way that was visceral, sexual and emotional. She wanted all the good stuff with every cell in her body. The stuff she hadn't enjoyed for decades. The stuff that made her skin tighten and her blood boil. She might easily have fallen in love with this man, but he wasn't ready for that, and he might never be.

That didn't diminish how she felt. She experienced all those wonderful things. But entering it with her eyes wide open was truly her choice. No one could accuse AJ Reed of using guile or manipulation to gain advantage. Honesty dripped off him. That only added to his appeal in her eyes.

Isla married young, and never fully understood the ways of the world and its people. Her ex wasn't a sleazeball, but she knew he could be one. He was a bit too slick for a salesperson and as the years passed, Isla tried to ignore how unattractive she found that side of him. Her ex wouldn't hesitate to shirk on a payment or argue with the wait staff and insist on seeing the manager of all the restaurants they frequented just to finagle a free meal.

She appreciated the straight shooting AJ from the first moment she met him.

And now? He was following her into her bedroom.

There were no words to describe the moment. She wished she had music, fireworks, or something else to commemorate such a turning point in her life. Something she never imagined happening again was about to take place.

His hand tightened in hers and her heart responded with an erratic beat. God, his strength, but she also sensed some insecurity in his grasp. It made her smile. This big bear of a man had such a sweet, funny, tender core. He melted her insides when he got nervous because of her. It was a heady sensation to feel desirable and sexy. For once, she was the aggressor to a beautiful man. Isla never thought of herself as someone who could make a man nervous.

Not this way.

She felt intoxicated by him.

They stopped next to her bed. Turning towards him, a small smile appeared on her face. He was in her bedroom. Her eyes reached his collarbone. Ignoring her nerves, she put both of her hands at the bottom of his t-shirt. Taking a deep breath, she slipped her hands under his shirt and felt the warmth of his skin that nearly singed her fingertips. His stomach rippled in response and he gasped. Lifting her eyes up to his, she slowly pulled his t-shirt off.

When she reached his shoulders, he moved his arms to

assist her and ducked his head. She drew in a gasp as she glimpsed his wide shoulders that were twice the width of her own, and his pecs and rippled abs flexed under his tanned skin. His chest hair was mostly gray and his skin was a bit looser than a man in his prime, but the sheer strength, beauty and physicality he possessed hadn't aged at all. He was, in a word, gorgeous. He was unbelievably attractive. Isla gulped and plumped up her confidence.

He was here with her, *he chose her,* didn't he? That was a pretty big deal. It meant everything to Isla. AJ Reed could not move on from losing his wife with just anyone. He would not allow just anyone to get close to him. This act of love was sacred to AJ and one he shared exclusively with his wife. To replace that image for him with a new one, herself specifically, was absolutely monumental in her eyes. *It said everything.* No fancy words to express their mutual attraction and desire were necessary.

His actions spoke much louder than any words could.

Isla didn't waste any time clucking over petty concerns about herself. Her stomach wasn't taut and tight like his was. Her thighs rubbed together when she walked and middle age gave her wrinkles and dimples on her knees. Her hair wasn't natural either. The morning would reveal how pale and drawn she was until she put some makeup on.

But AJ Reed, this man beside her, chose *her* tonight. He wanted her to be with him. For once, that was all the information she needed and would allow. Nothing more needed to be said. Isla saw a picture of his wife. Kate Reed was tall and exquisite.

But Isla wasn't her. And AJ wanted Isla now. At this moment. On this night.

Where would that lead? Was she merely an opportunity now, or a quick way to soothe his loneliness? Or was AJ just horny? Maybe all three. Of course he might have been. She accepted that the moment she opened the door to him. If that were the reason he came, she was glad for it.

Isla stepped closer and he tilted his head to gauge her next action. Her eyes were filled with longing and other things that need not be uttered.

He wanted to do this. He wanted her.

It was already more than enough to shore up any doubts or hesitation on her part. She would not deny herself the excitement, thrill, and beauty of what this night might be for her. She would not let any silly, petty, vain hang-ups over wrinkles and the ageing process interfere with what might turn out to be the greatest night she'd had in years.

That mattered to Isla.

She placed her hands just above his wrists and slid them upwards, letting her fingertips trail over the outside of his bare arms. The soft, subtle feel of the hair on his arms and the skin underneath made her tingle and all of her body parts tightened. She stood on her tiptoes to fully stretch and slide her fingers over his big, round shoulders and trace his jutting collarbone. Oh, the feel of him.

She had no plans. No idea how to proceed or what to do. She did exactly what she felt like. For the first time, she let her instincts dictate what to do. Releasing one hand, she surprised him when she circled her hand trail around his bicep before touching his back. The silky, soft skin over his tendons made her stomach jiggle with desire and a sexual attraction so deep, she had to catch her breath. She had no idea she could feel such thrilling sensations.

His wide back tapered down to where his jeans hung on him and his chiseled butt cheeks filled them nicely. She slid both hands down his back, trailing his spine, examining the valleys and planes. She barely touched and explored him, savoring the warmth under her hands. He shuddered and his head fell back when the ecstasy he so obviously felt emerged in a long moan.

She leaned closer, wrapping her arms around his middle and placing her lips on his back. Chills broke out all over him as her mouth touched and kissed him, slowly returning to his front again. She gently pushed him until he sat on her bed.

His gaze was fastened on hers now. There was a dark, deep expression in his eyes. No shyness or insecurity anymore. There was only a hungry urge now. For her. For her touch? Yeah, she had no doubt about it. Their gazes seemed suspended between them.

He put his hands on her waist; large, warm, capable hands that made her sigh with contentment. He pulled her forward, dragging her closer until she was straddling his left leg. Shocked by the sudden change, she blinked when she felt his leg pushing up. The pressure filled between her legs and an inferno of sexuality made her eyes widen as her wetness pooled. How long had it been since she felt that? Much too long. Their faces were only inches apart. His breath mingled with hers and their panting increased.

Pressing his leg and wanting more, she touched his face with her hand, cupping the side of his jaw. He leaned into her touch. She glimpsed the raw need that filled his eyes. She recognized the longing reflected in his gaze and it almost stole her breath away.

This man needed her touch. He needed to have a connection. He was aching for it. And now, Isla was aching for him.

She leaned forward and placed her lips on his. It was a soft kiss, one of exploring, discovering and sampling.

They kissed each other some more and she held his face between her hands, rubbing his cheek with her thumb, while he gripped her waist securely.

When his tongue entered her mouth, Isla was pleasantly surprised at how good it felt. The strong, warm, strokes made her whimper and she gripped his soft hair, wanting him to kiss her harder.

Their mouths meshed and they tasted each other like two starving people at a feast.

Her sleepwear was a basic pair of thin striped pajamas. He let go of her waist and slipped his hand up to her breast. Her tear-drop breast filled his palm and he liked the weight of it. Pushing the mound upwards, he familiarized himself with it by holding it firmly and brushing his thumb over her nipple. He repeated the action several times and the response by her body was instantaneous and all-consuming. Her hungry need began deep in the pit of her belly and streamed out down to her toes.

At that point, AJ took over. He lifted her body effortlessly and swept her off her feet. She found herself suddenly beneath him. Her head hit the pillow and his body half covered hers. He used his hands to move her into the right position and his lips only left hers when they had to. He sensuously licked her lips and peppered kisses all over her chin and neck, moving down with slow, languid repetition. He stopped to nuzzle her breast and took it fully into his mouth. It was mind-blowing and her entire body strained towards his.

Nothing mattered now but how he felt on top of her. His mouth, hands, and torso were heavy and crushed her a little but also filled all of her senses. He continued to kiss her while moving downwards to her stomach. He buried his face into her as if he wanted to suffocate himself. His need for her was definitely growing as was her need for him. Neither AJ nor Isla had any doubts. No insecurity. The glorious trust they both felt in wanting each other was phenomenal. She wanted him to see her, and touch her, and experience her whole body and nakedness.

His hands touched her waistband and she lifted her hips

to invite him further. He turned his head and made eye contact with her. The sweetness of his unspoken question totally melted the last of her reserves. He silently asked, *Is this okay?*

She nodded. "Yes. Please… AJ…"

He dropped his head and slid down her legs before stripping off the rest of her clothing. Isla loved feeling of his skin sliding against hers and she moaned until his mouth devoured hers again. She was more than ready for a wild ride.

She hoped it would be.

The next hot, sex-fueled kiss included both of them pushing and prodding each other. As they rocked together with their middles touching, his jeans were the only barrier left to cross. She whimpered and heaved herself against his hardness.

He slipped one hand with care over her breasts, moving down to her tummy and then her hips. He gripped her inner thigh and cradled her. His hand traced the soft, sensitive, tender skin of her inner thigh and she nearly purred with delight. Her head spun with colors and brilliant fireworks exploded behind her closed eyelids.

Her cries were genuine and loud. She lost all the inhibitions she formerly experienced while having sex during her youth. She never felt so liberated or sensuous.

He slipped his fingers inside her, finding her core wet and eager for his touch. She fell back, letting go of him as she simply clasped her hands overhead and prepared to receive him. Shutting her eyes, she let him build her suspense, climbing higher and higher to the crescendo, until it happened. No words or sounds were necessary.

She let his fingers explore her, bringing her up to the brink of a cliff that she hadn't reached in far too long. It was far too long to remember. She plunged into the swirling vortex of colors behind her closed eyes, in a volcano of explosions, yearning, energy, images, and desires that were years in the making. She temporarily lost all concept of time, space and reality.

When she finally opened her eyes, she blinked several times to see the ceiling of her bedroom. Yes, indeed, she was still lying on her bed.

But oh, dear God. Had her bed ever been rocked like this? Her entire body felt like plastic goo and she didn't care if it ever solidified again.

AJ was leaning over her, and staring down at her.

She licked her lips and he smiled. "You're spectacular, Isla."

His deep tone seduced her all over again and his eyes flashed with pure male lust. What happened when he used her name? When did hearing her name become something sensual? It was a sexy endearment now.

Kate was not there. Isla liked that too.

AJ was fully present with her. Here. And she sensed he liked it.

A lot.

She pushed his chest to let him know she wanted to sit up and they did so together. Her hands grew frantic as she struggled with the snap on his jeans. He seemed amused by her fumbling. "Need some help with that, darlin'?"

Oh, her city heart swelled when he called her *darlin'*. This hot, built, silver-haired, old cowboy who was previously broken and lonely, was now here with her.

AJ was hers.

For now.

She didn't even look up as she worked his pants loose and opened them up to grip him. His hot, hard, pulsating erection was primed *for her touch*. Her hands were shaking and her legs began to ache again.

She longed to devour the man who gave her these feelings. Finally.

This time, she would make him do as she wanted. He fell back and lifted his hips to let her pull his pants down his long legs and eventually off him. Then she grabbed his throbbing shaft between her hands and lowered her head until her mouth found him.

∼

SHE TEASED HIM AT FIRST, using her tongue to scribe circles around him. He groaned when her sweet, hot mouth overtook him. He reached out for her shoulder, hair, anything on her to convey the thrills that were flooding him.

Feeling. He was so full of feelings. He forgot what the rush felt like. Two years flew by since…

No. No names necessary. Names didn't matter.

Her mouth enveloped him and it was sheer ecstasy. He was back in the now. He liked these feelings.

They were fantastic.

It happened so fast, he felt like a sixteen-year-old having his first sexual experience. He had no idea how badly he needed this gift. This release, courtesy of Isla.

He gripped her hair and moaned but she kept her mouth over him while his hips jutted upwards, greedily hammering the roof of her mouth. Now he wanted to bury himself in the heat he felt between her legs.

Mustering up his will power, he lifted her up until her mouth finally released him and he placed her alongside him. Pulling closer so they were face to face now, side by side, and he entered the hot folds of her welcoming body. His brain could have been floating on ether. This was heaven. He sighed as the wonderful sensations percolated through him.

He hoped she'd never stop. He felt the relief he'd been seeking for more than two years.

He was fully connected, engaged, and present with her. With Isla.

Sex was completely unlike sex with Kate. It was okay though and he was actually glad it was so different. Shockingly different.

He shut his brain down. No comparisons. There was no reason to do that.

He rolled towards her, putting her on her back. He pressed into her so hard, the mattress bowed under the stress. The best part? She pushed back even harder.

Their bodies rammed and banged together while their mouths thrashed, kissed and sucked, each one fulfilling the other.

Her arms held him, shaking with pleasure at his thrusting. Her eyes all but rolled back in her head.

Unable to contain the powerful energy between them, they faced each other in exhaustion, there was no holding back and AJ fully exploded inside her.

It was moments later he blinked in shock after all the feelings that had surged through him.

AJ had someone new.

Someone else.

Someone that he wanted.

AJ had Isla.

CHAPTER 9

"DO YOU THINK ANYONE heard us?"

Isla's voice interrupted AJ's racing thoughts. There he lay, naked front and back, with a woman in his arms. His front was pressed against every inch of the skin on her back and he lifted his foot and let his toes slide down her calves. Isla responded with an almost undetectable, miniscule shiver that AJ felt as it traveled through her entire body. They were getting very close.

"You live alone in a huge brick building," AJ replied calmly. An odd feeling began to grow inside him. It was a gnawing strangeness, peppered with guilt, and also neediness.

He was proud when his voice sounded unruffled. He was with another woman, not Kate, and that panicked him. Why? Because he was so desperate for Isla. He liked holding her. He was more than ready to… do it all over again.

His body was already responding when she twitched and silence descended. After several long moments, Isla said, "No regrets, AJ?"

"None."

"Was it weird for you?"

He nuzzled the back of her neck. "Well, I didn't think so. But do you usually do sex differently?"

She snorted at his quip. "You know what I mean."

He sighed. Of course he knew. Isla was referring to Kate, his dead wife. This marked the first sex AJ had shared with another partner since she died. "No. Not weird. No regrets."

"I found it spectacular. I haven't felt so wonderful for decades."

I have. He didn't voice that to Isla however. AJ tensed, feeling obligated to say something similar. But he couldn't. No. He refused to make comparisons. He could never disparage Kate. Lovemaking was always spectacular between them.

He never dreamed the day would come when he'd want to have sex with another woman.

"You don't have to answer that. I'm sorry. I haven't had good sex for many years. The last years, Martin and I rarely got intimate and when we did, I didn't easily orgasm, which I blamed on my age. I thought that pleasure in life was all dried up, as unsexy as that sounds."

He kissed her hairline. "Nothing is over for you. You're sexy and amazing."

His words were almost as nice as his arms holding her.

When she moved again, she shocked him by reaching behind her back and adjusting him before sliding his hot erection inside her. AJ began rocking her gently, in a sensuous undulation that soothed her and was so unlike the frantic pace of moments before. It seemed like a long, slow climb up Mount Everest to view the entire horizon of the world below them. His body slid inside hers and their hearts and breaths seemed to be one. When they both released a long moan together, it was over.

Isla simply let him slide out before she turned over and snuggled back in his arms.

AJ shuddered as he wondered how to let her go? The thought of leaving her made him apprehensive. He dared not sink back into the lonely, black hole that his former existence had become. Although he had no regrets, which he feared this moment would bring, he couldn't deny his clinginess and he suddenly never wanted to be away from her again.

"Isla? Do you want me to go?"

"AJ, don't be stupid. Your grip on me is too tight for me to believe you want to go either."

"I don't want to. But what if…"

"What if what?" she prodded. "Say it. And be honest with me. We were honest about sex so let's stay that way when we talk to each other."

"What if this was just motivated by my loneliness?"

"I doubt that. No one could have had what we just shared because of only loneliness." Her laugh was refreshing and it comforted him. "There's hot chemistry mixed in with that loneliness."

"I came here strictly because I was lonely."

"You wanted to see me and I wanted you to stay. No one and nothing else mattered because of the chemistry that drew both of us together like a magnet. It was far more than your loneliness and grief. Right?"

The truth of her words made sense to him. "Damn… I think you're—"

"Right? Of course, I'm right."

"Are you asking me to stay?'

"Oh, god, yes. I want you to hold me so we can both rest up and then do it all over again before I open my eyes in the morning."

He chuckled and his heart lifted at the playful tone of her voice. "Which part?"

"All of it, AJ. I want it all." She turned to stare into his eyes. "How about you? What was it like for you? This was the first time since your wife died. Right?"

"Yes. It was. I used to try to imagine how I'd feel in this moment. But it wasn't anything like what I expected. The undertone of tragedy I thought would be here, isn't."

"Thank goodness, it wasn't like you imagined. Nothing sexy about that." He knew she was teasing, but her eyes were warm with excitement.

"It was hot and engaging and…"

"A reflection of us," she finished for him.

He let her words sink in. *Us*. He was part of something. He'd only ever been part of an "us" with Kate. But Kate wasn't here anymore. He couldn't hold Kate in his arms. The body he held in his arms was different than hers. Not better or worse. Just different. New.

Us.

"Yeah."

"Let's go to sleep. Wake me in the morning. Tomorrow is Monday, my day off, so I won't be getting up at my usual unreasonable hour. I plan to sleep in."

Go to sleep. Don't wake her except for sex. She made her needs known. His first time with this new partner could have been far worse, he supposed.

AJ slept like a log. Long ago, when he was a regular on the rodeo circuit, he could sleep that well. Being young, wild, and brimming with endless energy, he never stopped. AJ could fall sound asleep anywhere and anytime back then. Bull-riding was the most challenging skill and it never failed to give him a good night's sleep.

He hadn't slept so well since Kate got sick.

What did that mean?

Nothing. His heart insisted it was nothing. Sex was

always exhausting if you did it right and he wasn't as young as he once was. That's all.

Isla was a beautiful and good—no, a *great* friend.

AJ woke her just as she asked him to.

It was daylight and the time had come to release her warmth from his arms... and then what? Go back to his normal routine again? Go work on the ranch? Whichever ranch he chose?

He really didn't want to do that today.

Not alone.

But what else could he do?

∼

ISLA WATCHED AJ as the daylight filled the room, brightening the soft beige walls with early morning light. It was a luxury she rarely got to indulge. She stretched and her toes touched AJ just below his knees. Would she ever get tired of feeling his body next to hers in bed? She couldn't imagine that day ever happening. She rubbed her toes against his hairy calves and loved how small he made her feel.

His doubts, however, were visibly returning. Now that the sex was behind them, he started to doubt himself. Isla figured it made sense. She wasn't offended and decided to distract him. "Wanna try a new cupcake?"

"On your day off?" he asked as his eyebrows jutted upwards.

"Yep. I have a new recipe I want to try this morning." She stumbled around, looking for something to wear. The first thing she found was his t-shirt. Slipping it on, his scent engulfed her and her entire body reacted with a series of tingles. She already had it bad for this man. Her feet were cold so she opened her dresser and took out her pink, fuzzy socks, which she put on.

"Coming?" she called over her shoulder as she left the bedroom. She started to smile to herself when she heard him curse. He must have stumbled while getting out of bed. Isla was more than thrilled to have him here, in her very own home and place of business, preparing to bake cupcakes. The pure joy that filled her made her stop in her tracks.

It wasn't proper. AJ was neither her husband nor the father of her daughters. Nor her boyfriend. This encounter was random, completely beyond everything she always thought she wanted in life.

But it was exactly what she wanted now.

It took over half a century before Isla received that moment of perfection. No conditions. No expectations. Just the joy of being in the moment with a wonderful person.

When AJ appeared behind her, he was clad only in jeans, and she buzzed with excitement.

Giggling like a school girl drunk for her first time, Isla went into her bakery kitchen, barefoot and unprofessional, to gather the ingredients. Her shirtless, hot, hulking cowboy followed her and she barked out orders to him. As she expected, he did what she asked.

At first, he was perplexed by what she asked for.

His eyebrows rose at her last request and he asked, "That goes into a cupcake? Are you sure?"

She gave him a look. "Never doubt the ingredients of a genius. You'll see."

He handed her the jar of jam she asked for and when she took it, he suddenly grabbed her and tugged her forward, right against his chest, before bending down and pressing his lips on hers.

Startled by his action, she accidentally dropped the jar and it fell with a *thunk*. He pushed her forward until her backside hit the counter. Using her hands to brace herself, she bumped into the bag of flour, which also fell to the floor.

The puff of white powder that floated up created a fine dust. But that didn't stop AJ. He kept kissing her as his mouth drifted downwards and his hands inched upwards.

"You. On the counter. Now," he commanded as he lifted her. She was surprised, but heaved herself onto the counter. She reached for him but he batted her away. "No," he said and it thrilled her.

He pushed on her chest and she fell backward on the counter; then he pulled her bottom forward, and then... she got her own piece of heaven. His tongue touched her warm center and she nearly swooned.

She didn't care about the neighbors this time.

AJ quickly brought her to orgasm and she lay there breathless, as if she'd just completed a marathon.

She could barely manage to close her knees and when she finally opened an eyelid, she found him grinning at her. He looked with her with the swagger of a pirate. His hands were on his hips and his elbows were sticking out. But Isla could only stare at his hard-on that strained to get out of his jeans. "You're covered with flour," AJ explained.

She smiled and their gazes stayed fastened. "So are you."

"It looks hot on you. But not as hot as my shirt." He came forward and politely reached out before lifting her up. Isla felt like a rag doll in his huge arms.

He stole her heart when he leaned forward and planted a soft, sweet kiss on her forehead. It seemed apologetic. What was he sorry for? Giving her the most incredible moments of her life? He smiled and brushed her cheeks and hair with his fingers.

"Flour," he whispered softly at her questioning look. His hands reminded her of big paws on a lion. Gently placing her arms in his hands, he lifted her off the counter. Isla's feet touched the ground, but she was still shaky.

"Keep this up and I won't be able to walk," she quipped.

His expression dropped. "Did I hurt you?"

She glanced up and realized his devastation at the thought was real. She quickly grabbed his face in her hands. "No. Not at all. It's the most wonderful problem I could have. The best. Being sore from so much pleasure?" She waved behind her. "It's a dream come true."

"You'd tell me, right? If I get a little carried away? It's been… awhile…"

Well, okay, sure. If she got so sore that she couldn't walk for a week, that was fine. Stepping forward, she said, "I love the way you react to me and I'd tell you if I didn't like it."

"I appreciate that."

She stretched up on her tiptoes and tugged him down to kiss her. When their kiss ended, she said, "Keep this up and it won't be long before *you* can't walk."

"Is that a challenge?" his eyes sparkled with fun.

"No, it's an invitation for the next few days… weeks… or whatever it takes." Biting her lip, she hoped she didn't go too far. She had high expectations of this happening again.

He settled his hands on her waist and the expression on his face changed.

When he answered, the sexy lilt in his voice was absent. He said simply, "Whatever it takes."

Then he kissed her again. This time, it was much longer and more sensuous. She wrapped her arms around his neck and let the kiss speak for both of them.

She wondered what he felt and his words echoed in her mind… *whatever it takes*. That could mean so many things.

She hoped it meant lots more sex. She'd like more holding and snuggling too.

"Mother?"

The screech behind her made her freeze instantly, like having arctic water thrown all over her. The silliness, sexiness, and joyfulness vanished like ether in the wind.

She was a mother. And that was her daughter's voice.

Maggie.

Maggie was here.

In the kitchen.

Maggie saw her kissing a strange man with only a man's shirt covering her. And flour was everywhere. Isla was grateful Maggie hadn't walked in earlier.

Cringing in horror, she caught AJ's eyes as he instantly assessed the situation. He knew that voice when she screamed, *Mother.*

The screeching tone. A grown woman was standing in the doorway holding an infant.

Isla's daughter, Maggie.

Behind her, two little faces peeked out… Isla's granddaughters.

CHAPTER 10

"MOTHER?"

There it was again. That ear-piercing, shrill voice AJ first heard on the phone when he met Isla. Her unpleasant daughter. Obviously. Isla immediately reacted by shrinking in inches as if she collapsed into herself.

AJ stepped back and Isla spun around. Obviously, they were caught in a bad situation. Embarrassing, mostly. But that voice he heard screaming in the room had the same effect as fingernails on a chalk board, magnified by a hundred.

The moment was not ideal. Caught in the kitchen, they were both half-dressed with spilled flour all over the floor and on Isla. From her hair to her face and legs. AJ was sure he had it on him too. At least, they didn't walk in while AJ's face was wedged between her legs. So, there was that small comfort.

AJ fought the desire to step in front of Isla and tell her shrieking shrew of a daughter to leave them be and mind her own business. Isla was a grown woman who could kiss whomever she wanted to in her own kitchen. She was minding her own business in her own house and her own entire building actually.

But he feared he would appear inappropriate—maybe. Or was it something else?

The soul-crushing contagion that her daughter seemed to infect Isla with resumed in a flat second. AJ knew he could do nothing but observe.

"Maggie. I—I wasn't expecting—"

"Obviously. *Mother.* You weren't expecting us." The woman in the doorway snapped with gritted teeth.

AJ had to exit to avoid scolding the infamous Maggie before telling her to leave. He could never tolerate a daughter like Maggie. He touched Isla's arm. "I'll… uh… leave now." She looked up at him and silent messages emerged from her eyes. *Don't leave now. Don't go. Oh, my god. What should I say to her? I'm so embarrassed. Take me with you?* He could swear all of those messages were written in her gaze.

"Yes. Okay."

AJ left, dressed only in his jeans. Isla wore his shirt. He was unwilling to slip past Maggie to get his boots and socks. He trotted to his truck barefoot and bare-chested before quickly getting out of there.

Feeling like a jerk, he hated to leave the woman he'd been making love to and let her deal with the fallout alone but he knew his presence would only make things worse.

He cringed and mentally cursed. Having spent his youth basically riding bulls and always around ranch hands, he knew curse words that could make long-haul truckers blush. He didn't swear usually. Not until now.

By the time he arrived at the old Wade Ranch, he was calmer once more. Okay, so what if it ended badly? Maybe the daughter deserved to see her mother independent and free. Rip off the Band-aid and get it over with. Isla would have to confront her shrieking jerk of a daughter eventually and stand up for herself. She had to live her life as she chose to. She could do whatever she wanted now. She deserved to have everything she wanted because she lacked it in the course of her marriage.

He nodded as if he were speaking to someone. Yes. This would force the issue and maybe finally resolve something. It was time for Isla to do that with her daughter.

Gulping, he stared in horror at his front door when he pulled into the driveway.

There stood *his* daughter, Cami. She was standing on his door stoop, knocking loudly. Of course she was looking for him. The usual checkup. He should have anticipated her visit. But how could he know she'd come over instead of calling him?

Turns out... It was—entirely different though, when it came to his daughter.

She turned at seeing his truck approaching. Tilting her head and shielding her eyes from morning sun, she was clearly wondering, where did he go so early? He had no choice but to face her.

Sucking in extra air for courage, he reminded himself Cami was nothing like the shrieking Maggie. Cami was kind and sweet and understanding. Cami understood how life worked... so maybe...

No. No. No maybes. It was not okay.

It was only okay with her mother.

Isla wasn't his wife, or Cami's mother, or even AJ's girlfriend.

He should have left last night and been home when she came over.

"Where did you go so early? Did you get..." her voice trailed off as he exited the vehicle. His right barefoot was the first thing that came into her view. No missing that as he slid off the driver's seat in the dusty driveway. Luckily, the dust was powdery and soft on his bare feet.

Lord.

"Cupcakes?" Cami finished her thought as AJ fully emerged. Cringing. Blushing. Shameful. He wanted to bury himself in the dust.

Yes, he was trying to get some cupcakes ironically.

But not in the way his daughter thought.

"Um…"

Sighing, he looked heavenward and thought, *"Kate, if you were alive, I would not be standing half naked in front of our daughter before I break her heart and lose all of her respect for me. Not sure which is worse."*

"Dad? What happened?"

"I don't know how to tell you."

"Are you okay?" she immediately stepped closer to him. "What happened to your shoes?"

Did she wonder if he was going insane? Totally cracked from all his grief, did he wander through town shoeless and shirtless in search of his missing wife? In the past, the feeling that drove him to Isla could have been that strong, that compelling, and that deep. But Isla had a remedy for it.

Crap.

"I'm fine. I…" He sighed and shook his head. Meeting her gaze straight on, he threw his shoulders back. "I was visiting someone. And the circumstances required me to leave quickly and hence, my state of undress." He lost his guts and his gaze drifted away from her sincere, but shocked, sweet facial expression. He added, "I'm sorry, Cami, I'm really, really sorry that you had to find out this way."

Her eyes widened. "Visiting someone? Was it… a woman?"

"Yes." He finally faced her like the honorable father she thought him to be.

Her head tilted again. She shut her eyes and opened them. His heart ached when he glimpsed the pain that flashed in her eyes. "I'm sorry," he repeated.

Her eyelids fluttered open. "Oh, Dad. No. Don't be sorry. It's… natural… you…"

"No," he interrupted her. "No, there is nothing natural about it. I never planned this. I—I still love your mother as much as I always did. I just got…" He sucked in more air. This was harder than anything he had to tell her before. Harder than the first time he knew Cami was having sex and they had to discuss it. "Lonely," he finished weakly.

"You don't owe anyone an apology. You did nothing wrong. You're allowed to feel lonely and also happy. Is… it anyone I know?"

He wanted to tell her the truth. But he failed to this one time. "No." He wasn't ready to identify the other party. The whole experience was too fresh and too new to even process, let alone, find the right words to explain it to his daughter. A daughter that still actively grieved for her mother.

"Dad? Mom didn't want you to mourn for her the rest of your life. She told you to find someone when she's gone. You have to live still."

"I haven't found anyone." He responded too fast and too harshly. But the thought of not being Kate's husband in Cami's mind, and maybe in his own, left him in a panic. No. He wasn't committed to anything. He was still Kate's husband. He loved her still. But he also liked Isla. And the loneliness that plagued him since Kate died was hard to deal with.

"When you do, it'll be a good thing. I promise you."

"That won't happen so you don't have to worry."

"I'm not worried. I really mean it."

"So do I," he replied. Again, sounding far too harsh. She studied his expression and finally nodded.

"Okay, Dad. But if you ever do meet someone, I'd be very open and accepting."

He shut his eyes. His heart burst with pride over the his daughter's generosity and magnanimity. She would never shriek at him even if she knew what Isla's daughter knew. "You're an incredible light in my life, Cams."

"You're an incredible beacon in mine, AJ."

He finally met her gaze and her words caught him. The tone of voice she used to say "AJ" was a joke between them. When she first came to live with him, she called him AJ until it nearly drove him nuts. Now she only did it when she was teasing him. Her eyes sparkled.

He swallowed, not quite ready to smile over this. "Can you keep it to yourself and not tell your brother? Or anyone else? It's so new that I don't want to hear any outside comments."

"Of course."

She started to turn and leave. "Cams?" he called after her.

"Yeah?"

"You're really the best daughter I know."

"Absolutely true, I am. Glad you finally see that." She waved and left him alone. But this time, he was profoundly relieved. He couldn't wait to shower, wash off his night and recall all the images… before putting some clean clothing on.

The day was easy to fill. Always was. The chores were endless. Time-consuming and energy-sucking.

But evening always came. The sense of isolation returned no matter where he bunked and it dropped like an anvil on him every single night.

AJ hated feeling weak, but that night he didn't want to stay there. All day long, he debated and tried to rationalize his impulse. First, he told himself it was a onetime thing. Grief, isolation and horniness made him seek a natural outlet and he found one in an attractive woman his age. But that was all.

Then the gnawing feelings returned and he decided to check on Isla. That was all. No sex. Just checking on her to see how things went after he left. What kind of schmuck would he be if he didn't at least do that? But how the hell should he do it? Just by showing up? No. Calling? Texting? Not with her daughter there. Isla's shrinking demeanor and utter embarrassment were caused entirely by him. So what the hell should he do now?

~

"Who was that man?" Maggie demanded as she entered the messy kitchen.

Isla nodded. "Excuse me while I—"

"Put your clothes on?" she sniped.

Putting on her best smile, and seeing that her granddaughters were watching, Isla nodded as if it was perfectly normal. "Yep, girls, let me freshen up and then we'll chat and have some yummy cupcakes, okay?"

"Mom!" Maggie started to follow her like a cat stalking its prey.

She spun around and hissed at Maggie, "No, Maggie. The girls are here. We'll talk about this later."

"Mom you can't expect me to—"

"I can and I do. I expect you to act like an adult."

"But... who was he?" Isla sympathized just a bit when Maggie's gaze revealed her disbelief and pain at the question of *he*. The sole fact being he was *not* Maggie's father, no doubt.

"AJ Reed. He's a local cowboy and ranch owner. Does it help to know that? We'll talk later. I mean it, Maggie, when we're alone. Not in front of the girls. Now let me go and freshen up."

Isla raced up the back stairs and finally reached her apartment. She closed her door and leaned against it, nearly collapsing with exhaustion. She placed a hand over her thumping heart and took several deep breaths to calm down. Did that really happen? Despite her sharp retorts and self-control toward Maggie, internally, Isla felt exactly the opposite.

Maggie came to her bakery without any warning and saw her half naked with a strange man. Her little grandkids, ranging from only three months to eight years old, were with her and never mind what happened before they kissed and Maggie walked in on them.

What if they'd entered just a few minutes earlier? That might have been a moment she could not defend. The embarrassment and shock for all parties would be too much to bear. When she heard Maggie's shrill voice, Isla feared she did something that could severely alter her relationship with her daughter.

Rattled and self-conscious, Isla had no idea how to explain her overnight sex encounter. At this point, that was all AJ was to her. And possibly all he might ever be. He had to overcome his own past and hang-ups. But right now, as of today? They slept together and that was all.

Isla pretended to be cool in front of Maggie. But inside, a deep sense of shame began to grow.

Running upstairs to be alone was all she could think of to relieve it. She sighed and felt unforgiving disappointment in herself.

Could she ever be free to let go and get a little wild and crazy and decadent? Couldn't she have one full night of her own pleasure without fearing anyone else's criticism and denigration?

Nope. From here on out, her roles were exclusively a mother, a grandma, and an ex-wife.

Last night was unplanned and wonderful and Isla resented the fact that she could not be all alone in her own establishment. Maggie intruded into *her* space so rudely and presumptuously that she felt like she'd done something wrong.

What were the chances one of her daughters and grandchildren would show up on this particular morning of all mornings?

Trudging into her bedroom, she stopped and stared at the bed. The twisted covers evoked sensuous images. They needed a good washing from all the things she did with AJ last night. For a moment, Isla felt greedy.

She'd never been greedy in her life. And didn't she deserve to feel that way for at least twelve hours?

Nope. Apparently, not. Karma and the universe conspired to foil her greediness.

She ducked into the shower and quickly scrubbed herself while remembering her decadent night. Coming out, she continued her grooming by habit and the ensuing boredom she felt made her fight the impulse to scream.

Or bang the side of her head on the wall.

Or tease her hair up and wear thick makeup with glitter to be someone entirely new and different.

Last night, she got to be someone else, someone new and shiny and sexy. She resented that she so soon had to stop being that woman. Isla wasn't ready to give that up.

And all because her freaking daughter showed up?

After a lifetime of doing what people expected from her, Isla finished styling her hair in the same way she'd worn it for ten years. Slipping into her clothes, she took AJ's shirt and put it into the laundry basket.

She picked up his boots and socks, setting them beside

her bedroom door. For now, they would stay safely in her domain. Her sanctuary. Her landmark of the most personally fulfilling night of her entire life. Even sex when she was young was never so good for her.

AJ? Isla guessed it wasn't the same way for him. His marriage sounded strong until the end. He was extremely practiced at sex. Excellent skills. Epic, actually.

They were too old to worry about what got them together at this age and influenced them. The fact that they both had freaking grandkids certainly made it different. Not like sex in your twenties. The fear of being walked in on by your parents didn't compare to being walked in on by your grandchildren. Hard to feel sexy with that realization.

Isla regretted how abruptly it ended. No chance to make a date to see each other again, or not. She wanted to say goodbye just to get an inkling of what he was thinking about it. And what he wanted to do now.

But poor AJ heard Maggie's screech and that was enough to usher him out. Isla wished she had a chance to encourage him to come back, if only to keep him from freaking out. She knew his wife was weighing heavily on his mind. Guilt? Regret? Sadness? Probably those and more. He'd been clear about his love for Kate and probably believed he'd never want another woman's touch again. The shock of doing something so unlike himself must have also been on his conscience.

Considering what happened last night and this morning —well, Isla hoped the chance he could turn skittish did not have good odds. She knew she wasn't being overly confident but no one could deny the explosion of feelings that they shared last night.

Squaring her shoulders, Isla descended the stairs and returned to the kitchen. Shaking her head, she observed the spilt flour and imagined she'd be sweeping up the fine granules for months to come. It could have been fun to clean up with AJ still there.

Now, it was just another chore she had to get done. Check off another box. Until last night, that was all she looked forward to in this new life she created. She liked living alone. But she loved to make progress and proudly tick off her to-do list.

Until last night. Now? Even that little thrill seemed stale compared to last night.

Maggie and the kids were in the seating area of the shop. Peeking out for a moment, Isla watched them. Her heart started to melt a smidgeon for resenting them at first.

Maggie stood there, her newest baby, Taylor in a sling as she swung her unconsciously, back and forth in a soothing moment. The three-year-old was contentedly smashing up a cupcake that formerly had a mini-castle shape. Now it was a pile of chocolate crumbs that looked entirely inedible but Carrie seemed delighted with it. The eldest child, Caisley was coloring a picture as she bit off a piece of her cupcake which was shaped like a rainbow.

The four of them looked beautiful together with their matching blond hair and pale features that replicated Isla's. Maggie looked just like Isla. But right now? Maggie's face was contorted with unhappiness. To be fair, Isla imagined if she'd caught her own mother being intimate with a man, even her own father, she'd probably have the same response that Maggie had.

But AJ wasn't her father.

That tripled the trauma of it. Maggie was taking her parents' divorce the hardest. Her ideals of marriage and family were founded in the childhood she remembered and loved. She often told Isla she wanted to raise her children that same way that Isla and Martin raised her.

So Maggie's entire foundation was blasted away. She

observed the distance that was growing between Isla and Martin but never dreamed they would actually divorce and make it official.

Plastering a smile on her face, Isla entered the room. "So, what do I owe this wonderful surprise to? Aren't you girls still in school?"

"Hi, Nana. Yes. We got to take a little break." Carrie answered, her childish voice squealing.

Glancing towards Maggie, Isla raised her eyebrows curiously, wondering why Maggie would bring the girls here while school was still in session. The kitchen scene might have been unexpected for Maggie and the girls to walk in on, but it was Monday and Isla had no way of predicting the unannounced visit of her daughter. Maggie turned her head and stared out the window, purposely ignoring Isla's searching gaze.

Finally, she turned around, still avoiding Isla's piercing look. Odd. Seemed like something more was bothering her besides seeing her mother kiss another man. What was it? It seemed obvious now but it had to wait for later. First came the kiddos. "Well, since this is a day for wonderful surprises, what do you say we go bake something yummy?"

"There's a mess in the kitchen."

"So there is. But white flour on the floor never hurt anyone. Come on. Let's go design our own desserts." It was something Isla had been doing with Caisley since she was a toddler and now Carrie followed her. Maggie, however, did not seem interested.

Isla let it go. Hours later, after baking with the girls and finally cleaning up the mess she and AJ made, it seemed like eons since he was there. Isla's baking area was back in order.

She was still exhausted from the previous night but she ignored it, trying her best to keep up with the girls. They brought suitcases filled with stuff and duffel bags and their favorite toys. Noticing the copious amount of luggage they carried, Isla had to wonder just how long they planned to stay. Then came the million dollar question: why? Why did they show up all of a sudden?

It was after dinner and the girls were all bathed and in bed. The baby was snuggled into her portable bassinet when Isla finally sat down across from Maggie.

"So who goes first? Me or you?" Isla's old way of dealing with her daughters was no longer useful. She previously liked to prod and poke, kind of tap dancing around them to detect their moods. Not this time. She remembered the things AJ said after he heard Maggie speaking to her. The selfishness and rudeness still blared loudly in her brain.

Maggie evil-eyed her for too long. She was trying to strong arm Isla into apologizing. NO. Damnit. This was *her* house. The entire building was hers and hers alone. Isla was completely justified in doing whatever the hell she chose to do. She had sex with a man who was single and there was no shame from either party. None. Maggie had no open invitation to invade her space and well, hell. Isla could have sex on her kitchen counter before serving breakfast if she so desired.

"Who is he?" Maggie asked in a dull tone.

"I told you already. He's a local rancher."

"Are you dating him?" she growled.

"I don't know, Maggie. Last night was a first for us."

"As in—"

"Yes, we had sex. I'm divorced; I'm not dead yet. Some men even find me attractive. And let's not forget: your dad divorced me. But in all fairness, it was overdue." It should have happened long before but she refrained from lambasting Maggie with brutal honesty.

"You were... wearing his shirt. Only his shirt."

Isla straightened her back and smiled. "Yeah, Maggie. So what if I was?"

Maggie tilted her head and stared at her mother in disbelief. "You're not sorry?"

Isla couldn't stop her grin. "I'm really not. So there you go. That's about it. He was my first customer and he's been coming here every morning since. We started chatting naturally as he was often the only one here. Eventually, I learned he was a widower and still grieving. Not looking for anyone to date. So we agreed to be friends. But in all honesty, I wanted more. Then, somehow it just happened. No more details."

Maggie swallowed. "Wow. I never thought—"

Her gaze stopped her daughter. "I know you didn't. I didn't for a long time either. But it's time to move forward. Your dad did. And it's my turn now. You expect me to be a saint? Why would you have higher expectations for me? Should I remain frozen in time while he gets—"

Isla's anger sparked as she spoke, recalling the last few years and Maggie's odd behavior regarding what made her mad at Isla versus her dad.

But suddenly, Maggie made an awful face before she bent forward and began to cry. Hard and loud. Startled, Isla could only watch her in shock.

Finally, she moved next to Maggie and began rubbing her shoulder. Maggie suddenly turned and grabbed her, pressing her head against her mother like she used to do as a little girl when she got scared or hurt.

Patting Maggie's sprigs of curls, Isla said softly, "What happened, honey?"

"George. He... he left me. Us. He's been having an affair. And now he's... gone. Gone. I came here because I didn't know where else to go. He's not the man I thought he was." Maggie's sobs overtook her and she looked up. "I have three kids to raise, and one of them is a newborn, Mom. What'll I do?"

Oh, lord. this was so much more than Isla was prepared for. She patted and soothed Maggie with optimistic words, letting her cry while she tried to think of solutions. When her crying slowed, Isla suddenly realized how upsetting this morning must have been for Maggie. She was already hurting when she got there and then to see her divorced mother looking happy with another man?

Yeah, worst timing *ever*.

The news was still registering in her mind. George left? He was having an affair? George was an engineer who had worked for a large firm for a long time. He was solid, decent and kind of dull in a nerdy way. Why on earth would he leave Maggie? Maggie was considered by many, but not Isla, as being *out of his league*. And yet, *he* cheated on *her*?

"Tell me what happened, honey."

Maggie spent the next several hours going into the weeks that led up to last night. She had no idea what happened. She got a goddamned text message from George that came from a city hours away. Isla asked to see the text before she could believe it. George ended ten years of marriage to Maggie and three kids with a text? He literally ran away, and for two days Maggie worried where he went. Then she received that terrible communication from him. She was still taking care of his three daughters.

Isla stopped worrying about her own life and AJ and held Maggie when she broke down sobbing again. "What am I going to do, Mom?"

"You can live here. You and the girls can stay here with me. That's what you'll do."

Isla fully committed in that second. Nothing came before her kids. And it was a comfort to realize that part hadn't changed about her.

AJ sat down on the bench and stared at the river. He remembered sitting there with his son, Asher and helping him figure out that he loved Daisy. AJ had been sitting there for decades, staring at the bend in the river that lay below the Rydell family beach.

He watched the river ripple and lap for all those years. So many sunrises and settings each day. From snow to heat, and new growth to falling leaves, to smoke and suffocating wildfire. Fire had become the fifth season around River's End now between each summer and early fall.

AJ watched it all in the years he'd been living there.

He sat on this bench after his wife died. He remembered how much his heart was aching. He wanted to die. He relived those moments as well. Grueling, exhausting, dark moments of grief, pain, and trauma. His desire to leave here was only outweighed by the puzzle of how to achieve that task. He missed his wife.

He loved his wife. His Kate. He always would.

But something new and strange was happening. He discovered his heart was still beating in his chest. He had new words and thoughts to analyze and share. What happened today was awesome. In this present day.

Two years *after* Kate died, he found new things to say. New things to laugh over. New experiences to share with a new woman.

Kate was unavailable.

But Isla wasn't.

He once thought those feelings and desires were long dead and buried. His life became his work, his kids and his grandkids. They were enough. More than most people had. More than he had before Kate.

But now?

It wasn't enough. He made a friend. And found a lover. And now he missed her too. Isla had a different identity when he wasn't with her. Different from Kate. But AJ missed Isla now.

He loved Cami and Asher, his two children. They were years apart in age, personality, temperament and lifestyles. AJ loved both of them equally and with all of his heart.

Could that same theory of love be applied to spouses? Dead ones and new ones? Could it be the same logic? Could you love more than once in a lifetime?

It pained him to answer the question. The iron resolve he once felt over Kate's grave when he said his last words to her haunted him. As he knelt over her and prayed and cried, he vowed that he would never love anyone but her.

Ever.

The end.

It was supposed to be the end of his story too.

But, when life went on, day by day, things changed and so did he… His previous resolve became burdensome and limiting. Then it became much too heavy to bear.

What if his old heart had enough room for another?

Someone like Isla?

CHAPTER 11

*C*RAP. AJ'S DAUGHTER. SHE was Isla's first customer a few mornings later. Already exhausted from the last two nights, Isla wasn't ready to deal with her. But instead, she smiled as she rang up Cami's cupcake order.

"How are you?" Cami asked as she handed some change to Isla.

"Oh, good. Business is picking up. Only because of your generous family. Can't be grateful enough."

"That's good to hear. I've already gotten used to having your bakery here and I'd be heartbroken to lose your cupcakes not only to eat but also to bribe my teenagers to do stuff for me. They'll do just about anything they're so much in love with them."

Isla's heart swelled. AJ's twin grandsons. Yep, she knew them. She saw them in there often eating two cupcakes a piece. They didn't pay much attention to her but were always polite in the store.

"Everything okay? You look a little tired." Cami asked. Isla glanced up to find Cami tilting her head and watching her.

"Oh. My daughter came into town unexpectedly Monday morning, and well, things didn't go as planned."

"Oh. Are those your grandkids?"

Isla glanced at a corner table where the older two amused themselves. Maggie was rocking the baby on a chair. "Yes."

"They're adorable." Cami glanced to her grandkids. But her gaze came back sharply on Isla. "So they showed up Monday morning, huh? Was it early? Wake you up?"

"No. I was awake. I started the day off by spilling the flour everywhere and it was just… a very long day. Not as young as I used to be. I guess it shows too."

Cami was studying her and tilted her head. "Actually, I bet most people don't think you look like a grandma. Funny. You're not the only one who had such a strange morning. I stopped by my dad's Monday and his was a pretty strange morning too. But he went so far as to lose his shirt and boots. Any chance you might know where they are?"

Isla froze and the blood literally drained from her face. "You were there when he got home?"

Isla prepared for Cami to shove the freshly frosted cupcake in her face. Then she imagined Cami would rush over to commiserate with Isla's resentful daughter.

Instead, Cami started to grin. "Oh, yes. He hasn't told you yet? He got out of his truck dressed only in his jeans, looking a bit horrified when I asked him how he managed to lose most of his clothing at such an odd time of day. He blushed to his toes. I kept wondering who it was until… just now. Your mixed up morning kind of matches my father's."

"He didn't tell you what happened?"

"He said something new was happening and asked me to keep it quiet, which I will, Isla. I'm sorry I teased you just now. I couldn't resist when I finally connected the dots."

"You're not upset?"

"Of course not. He's a grown man. And single."

"He suffered a lot these past few years since losing your mom." Isla said simply. Unsure if that was wrong to say.

"Yes." Cami's tone was soft as was her sad smile. "Endlessly. If you can ease that, I'll welcome it."

"We haven't decided anything."

"Well, I suspect you have but he might not have the words to explain it. I doubt he even knows how to date. When he and my mom met, I think my mom pursued him, not the other way around. Here's a valuable tip. If he seems careless, it's probably because he doesn't know what to do. Or else it's guilt. There's a bit of that going on there too."

Isla's eyes widened. "Are you rooting for this to continue?"

Cami gave her a soft smile. "I'm rooting for my dad's happiness. And if that means you? Then yes. I guess you know about my mom. I expected him to tell you about her before he considered anything beyond her. But yes. I'll keep your secret, and stay out of it. I won't corner you or put you on the spot again. I'm sorry. Again, I just ran with the moment and couldn't wait to crow about my sleuthing skills. That morning must have been pretty dramatic. I admit I was seriously curious."

"Cami, I'm not sure how to respond to that."

Cami grabbed her order, flashing a grin a she turned to leave. "You don't have to say anything, Isla. I'll see you next cupcake run. My husband is addicted to them now too, so it'll probably be tomorrow."

Isla muttered a goodbye as Cami sat down at a table. The line got longer and Maggie was useless, sitting unhelpfully in daze so Isla had to keep going. AJ got caught by his daughter too. Who could imagine such beautiful irony? Isla guessed Cami's reaction was much milder and less dramatic than Maggie's.

What could Isla do next? How could she progress forward?

~

"I'm coming back from Anderson's ranch. Let's meet at the cupcake shop in town. Eleven is the only time I can make it," Mack Baker informed AJ. Grimacing at Mack's choice, AJ sighed internally.

Four days had passed since his wild, amazing, erotic and out of character night occurred. Both of their daughters discovered them and AJ didn't know how to feel about it. Worse still, he didn't know what to say to Isla now.

Should he call? That seemed old-fashioned. Text? That seemed too faceless and hard to convey what he meant. What the hell should he do? Show up at her place again? What if she thought he assumed he could just do that? Show up for sex whenever the urge came as if they were geriatric booty calls?

If not that, what were they doing? And were either of them ready to call it anything more? AJ needed three foremen and he had to have a conversation with Mack. He also needed to man up and have a conversation with Isla.

"Yeah. Okay. When you get there, tell Mrs. Whitlock the tab is on me. See you soon."

Tell the woman he recently had sex with before he ghosted her that he was paying. Was that the right term? He had no idea how to pursue a woman. None. At all.

He honestly didn't remember ever having to. Women used to wait in line for one-night stands with AJ when he rode bulls on the rodeo circuit. Prison came next and when he got out, he changed his entire life. First, he became celibate, then religious. Then Kate found him. Kate made it so easy for him that all he had to do was say yes.

This wasn't like that. Obviously. AJ had no clue how it would be.

His nerves stirred up the acid in his stomach, which began dissolving his stomach lining but AJ tried to appear casual when he entered the cupcake shop.

The bell overhead tinkled his arrival. The crowd was hopping and the tables were filled. A line formed for those who were ordering. It was a definite contrast to the quiet mornings they shared when he used to come in.

The place was becoming a hip hangout spot. Lots of people came just for the heavenly coffee Isla brewed. Others because of her unique flavors and variations of cupcakes and cookies.

Mack was already there and he waved to AJ. Glancing towards Isla, AJ knew at once she hadn't realized he entered her establishment. How would it affect her? Would she care? Did he want her to care? Would she be embarrassed? Mad? Confused? He was unsure. That was the only feeling he had.

"How's it going, AJ?" Mack asked as he walked up to him.

"Fine. Busy with the new ranches. Keeping me pretty much on my toes."

"You want to order? There's Ty over there and Justin will be a few minutes late."

"Yeah, let's do that." AJ loved leaving it to Mack to coordinate everything to his satisfaction. Mack was primed for a job as the supervisor and Tyrone and Justin could be foremen. The job titles were irrelevant. They all worked well together and they all knew their jobs. AJ didn't care what they called themselves as long as they did the work so he could manage the chaotic chores that also needed to be done. AJ was stretched too thin to adequately maintain the four ranches. Asher took care of the fifth one.

Swallowing hard, he turned to face the reception counter. The line had dwindled to just one ahead of him.

Finishing up, Isla smiled politely as she handed the drink tray to her customer. Her smile was soft and warm. It kept burning slowly and long inside his chest. Isla added light to the darkness that clouded his mind since Kate died. She was so different to look at than Kate. It was entirely strange and he also liked the newness of his feelings. He kept trying to analyze them. Did it hurt? Did he like it? Was it right?

At that moment, her gaze landed on his face. Her smile faded and weariness filled her expression. Her small posture straightened up in height. She waved her hand, indicating he should move forward. Order something. That was when he froze up.

Do something.

The last few nights he spent alone were darker than the previous whole years' worth.

Stepping up to the counter, his mouth went completely dry. "Hello, Isla."

Her eyebrows lifted. "Hello, AJ." Her lips compressed and she tilted her head to let him read the expression in her eyes: was he serious?

Clearing his throat, he shook his head, "How'd it go?"

"How'd what go?"

"You know." He didn't miss her incredulous tone laced with anger. She was moments away from lambasting him. He deserved it. Her eyes darted around to the corner table where her daughter and grandkids had set up camp. The raucous crowd in her shop kept her quiet.

"It was awkward, uncomfortable and terrible. About the same as it went with your daughter, I guess. She came in and asked about you and me."

His dry throat turned to a solid lump. "She didn't mention that. How was she... okay?"

"She was quite lovely. We both had a laugh about it. She

promised not to tell anyone. Quite a contrast to my daughter."

His shoulders shrugged. "Yeah, that sounds like Cami."

He flinched. Cami wasn't a jerk so he obviously wasn't about to compare her daughter to his. Not the way to score any points.

"She also cautioned me not to think of you as a bumbling ass when it comes to dating. I'm beginning to see how well she knows her father."

"She did not say that."

"No. Not exactly. But that was the gist and I know why she said it now."

The doorbell chimed and Justin walked in. Cringing in annoyance, AJ looked back and said, "I'm having a meeting right now, trying to hire some foremen. What if I come over tonight after work so we can talk?"

"Do you want to talk? Or do you prefer we have sex? Why now? Why not three days ago?"

Bristling, he gave her neutral look. "I told you I wanted you to be my friend. I was honest about it from the start. Things have changed but I'm still being honest."

She gave him another glare. "You can't come by like before. My daughter and kids are here now. Indefinitely. They need a place to live…"

Well, that sounded long and dramatic. Family problems. He had his own so they weren't hard to recognize. Glancing over, AJ noticed the baby. "How many kids do you have?"

Isla suspected he was calculating his own involvement with them. Through gritted teeth, she answered him. "Three."

"Three kids. How many grandkids?"

"So far, just the three. But don't be a damned idiot, AJ. You have grandkids too so let's not start celebrating all of their birthdays." She nodded over his shoulder. "They're coming over here. Order something quickly."

AJ swiftly obeyed her instructions and was more than eager to get out of line and away from Maggie's angry glare. Isla served AJ his usual, the only difference being the flavor and decoration on top.

He was fascinated by her endless imagination. He even took several pictures of her miniature masterpieces. Except for a few pictures of his grandkids, her cupcakes were the stars of his film roll.

Today's concoction looked like a real cactus. The bottom half of the cupcake appeared to be a small planter. He nodded as he handed her his credit card. "I'm buying for the entire table."

"That's generous of you. Like a date."

Frowning, he finally glared at her. "Point taken."

"Good." She smiled sweetly as she ran the card before handing it back to him. "I'll keep it open until they order and bring you the receipt. Next?"

She dismissed him with a smile, that was oh-so-big and generous but she directed it at Justin behind him. AJ glumly took his order and returned to Mack. They made small talk for a few more minutes until Justin and Tyrone ordered and finally sat down. As promised, Isla brought the receipt and dropped it on the table without a word.

Mack glanced at AJ than at Isla as she sashayed away. He could have sworn there was an emphasized wiggle in her butt. Mack tilted his head. "What did you do to piss off Mrs. Whitlock? She's got to be the nicest woman in town."

"We disagreed in how to raise our daughters." No one took criticism of their offspring well.

Justin snorted as he slid his chair back before sipping his coffee. "She's kinda hot in a motherly kind of way. Not like any granny I've ever seen though."

"Well, she *is* a grandma. That's her daughter and those are three of her grandkids." AJ said while indicating the corner table. Grumpily.

Justin looked over and whistled. "She's hot too. Crap, they're like twin versions of each other separated by a few years."

AJ didn't like his comparison or that they were talking about Isla. Maggie too, for that matter.

Mack glanced over his shoulder. "Yeah. The littles look like them too."

"Wouldn't get too interested. She can shriek like a cat caught between a Rottweiler's teeth," AJ said.

Mack laughed. "Not a fan, huh?"

"Not really. She's just yells a lot. Anyway, back to the reason I called you three here."

Mack's gaze lingered for a moment on Maggie, then whipped back to AJ. "Yeah. What is it?"

"I want you to come work for Reed Ranch Enterprises. As foremen. I'm offering all of you a pay raise, better benefits and lodging at the ranches."

Startled, they all three stopped moving and stared at him. Justin stopped sipping the straw, Tyrone broke off a piece of cupcake and held it mid-air, while Mack tilted his head curiously. "What about Jack, Ian, Ben or Pedro? What would they have to say?" Mack asked.

"Jack knows. I wouldn't have asked you without telling him first. They can't offer all three of you promotions. So I asked him and he agreed they could find other workers. But I can't find foremen like you guys anywhere."

Tyrone nodded, and a smile lit up his face. "Damn. That's the truth."

"Yeah, it is. As soon as you're ready to start, I have a list for each place about a hundred items long. You'll be fully in charge and hiring your own crews. Run any alterations or large purchases by me, but otherwise, you're on your own."

Justin whistled. "Damn. That's generous, AJ. And what about you?"

"I've got so much paperwork along with my own list of chores that I'll be busy for months to come."

"Jack really is cool about this?" Tyrone tilted his head.

"Yeah. He really is. And it's not because he feels sorry for me."

Mack gave him a long look. "I was actually thinking that."

"I know you were. He agreed this is the best opportunity for you three. He does see that."

"It really is." Mack said enthusiastically.

AJ slid a slip of paper to each man. "You'll get raises and be on salary, because that's what I think you're all worth."

Mack picked up the slip of paper, looked at AJ's face and then back down at the paper. He whistled. "You sure about this?"

"Completely. I'm up a creek if you decline. I have too much on my plate right now and I can't do it all."

Mack asked, "Then why did you buy all those ranches?"

AJ shrugged. "To bury myself in work. It was my therapy to get through some days."

Mack nodded, holding his gaze. "Fair enough. You had to stay busy. Has something changed?"

"No." Maybe. He glanced at Isla who was ducking down and searching the display for some dessert or another and he looked back at the men at the table. No. Nothing changed. "It just gets to be too much sometimes."

"Damn, AJ, I'm in." Justin said with a smile before giving him a fist bump. AJ responded with one of his own.

Tyrone suddenly stood up. "Hell yeah, I'm in too." He did a weird dance while Mack rolled his eyes and threw his napkin at him. Justin snickered and proceeded to join him in the fun.

AJ shook his head and a smile brightened his face. "Everyone is looking over here. Okay, enough. I get the message, you accept my offer."

"You're for real about all of this?" Tyrone stopped, still standing.

"Real as I can be."

Mack stood up. He leaned over and set his hand on AJ's. "Thank you, AJ. Where do we get started?"

Mack was a go-getter and needed no fanfare or hesitation. AJ made a wise choice to appoint him the supervisor, even if Mack didn't fully realize it yet. AJ brought out a notebook. "Let's talk about all the ranches and decide who fits best in which one. We can start there."

"We get to fucking live on them too?"

"Yes. I can't live on all four of them and Asher has the last one. But he needs help too. I bought acerage next to Asher so it's doubled in size now. That's the fifth ranch. So you're welcome to stay there if you don't mind sharing some of the responsibilities."

"They call his place Sugar Hill Ranch, right?"

"Yes."

"Yeah, damn. I'd love to stay there. The country up there is breathtaking."

Far nicer than the ranch where AJ worked. Justin snorted. "Nah. Too many hills to navigate with all those deep ravines and dry creek beds. Give me the old Wade place. Flat and easy. What do you say?"

"Fine by me. Tyrone?"

"Well, let's hear the other choices."

"Moon River Ranch or Rattlesnake Ridge Ranch. Come let's go check them out." AJ rose up as the guys did. They carefully separated the garbage from the recycling and slid the trays on top of the garbage while AJ stole a glance at Isla.

He walked over to her quickly. "I'm hiring these three men and I'm leaving now to show them my properties. But I want to finish our conversation. Where?"

Isla seemed to consider saying no, but finally, she nodded. "I guess at your place."

He shifted his weight from one foot to the other. She noticed him fidgeting and sighed, "What?"

"I don't really have a place. I usually bunk down at the old Wade Ranch. It's a work in progress. You could come by of course, but it's not very nice."

She gave him a look. "I'm sure it's fine. Text me the address."

He frowned. "You're going to drive out to see me?"

"Yes. I can drive a car and I know all about traffic signals and everything." Her sarcasm made him give her a dirty look.

"I didn't mean it like that."

"Then what?"

"I feel bad. I should come to you."

Isla glanced off towards the corner. "Yeah, I don't need that right now. Text me."

He retreated and left. The guys were waiting for him. They piled into AJ's truck, their spirits high. All of them were getting raises and a place to live that didn't include sharing quarters with anyone else or salvaging old trailers.

It turned out to be a productive day and they decided where each man would be based. AJ provided the lists for each ranch and showed them where they were located. The three men were very resourceful and didn't need any hand-holding to make it all work.

The last ranch was still being renovated so for now, that was mostly his domain.

AJ pulled into the old Wade place. Justin's future home.

That meant he had to move somewhere else. He still owned a perfectly lovely and beautiful house. In fact, for more than thirty years it was his and Kate's pride and joy. He raised a few horses on the ample acreage and customized several barns. It was a measure of his success. When Kate died, AJ rented it out. He bounced around at his son's place for a while and then started buying ranches.

Now?

He was bouncing again.

He could move back to his old house, but he knew in his gut he'd never do that. There was no day he'd move back into the house Kate died in. It would continue to be a source of income, and maybe someday, one of his grandkids might want it. But as for him? That chapter in his life was over. Done. Dead.

It all ended with Kate.

With a long sigh, he realized so much of his life ended with her.

But he was going to his current home, to wait for Isla. Oddly it seemed maybe new things were starting.

If he could figure out what to say *and* what exactly he wanted.

He dropped his coat and keys, glancing around with a wince. The place was old and in dire need of updating. He never bothered to care for it. AJ wasn't a total mess, but it wasn't like Isla's building. But it would have to do.

Then came the knock. She was here. With him.

CHAPTER 12

AJ SPRANG TO HIS feet and his stomach tightened painfully. Had it always been so hard for him with new people? Seemed that way. He never knew what to say to new people. That hadn't really changed. Kate encouraged him to feel confident for years, and his work involved all kinds of people with all kinds of personalities. It should have worked to make his communication skills stronger. But nerves still plagued him.

He walked across the room and opened the door.

Isla was standing there and AJ's heart pounded loudly. How pretty she looked in the evening twilight. Her hair cascaded over her shoulders. A strand was stuck to her lip gloss. She wore soft, pastel colors with warm hues like her personality.

"If it's just sex you want, then say so. I might be interested," she finally said when he just stood there staring at her.

"I haven't thought about just having sex for forty years."

"That's a long time, I suppose. But it's okay now."

"I don't know what I want. It's hard to move forward when I sometimes still forget my wife is dead and start to text or call her. Can you imagine what that's like to live with?"

"I can't. But do you think I could come inside regardless?"

Startled, AJ suddenly realized he forgot to ask her inside. Frustrated at himself, he sighed and ran his fingers through his hair. He was once blond but his hair was all silver now. At least he was lucky he didn't lose it, like a lot of fair-haired men. His hairline had slightly receded but it still existed.

"Of course you can. I'm sorry." He opened the door and she brushed past him. Only her elbow grazed his chest as far as any contact but that's all it took. AJ's body flinched and tightened as he fought the urge to grab her. Should he hug her? Press her against the door? What did she expect from him? The overwhelming rush of feelings left him with no idea what to do next.

Isla seemed oblivious to his suffering and she casually dropped her purse on a table. With a swift glance around the room, she said, "It's not as bad as I imagined."

"Thanks, I guess." He slammed the door shut.

Her gaze roved over him. "How'd your meeting work out?"

He crossed his arms over his chest. Her words seem innocuous enough, but her tone was pissed off. "Very well, thanks for asking. I hired three foremen. They'll help me manage my new empire."

"Are they all you need?"

"Basically, yes. They're the best in the area and they know all the best subcontractors. Each ranch is different and needs different repairs and material, so having them in charge will help me a lot. I can delegate most of the detail work to them, which will allow me to oversee it, instead of doing all the repairing and remodeling myself. As of right now, I'm literally nailing the fences back together to keep the animals from wandering as well as feeding, tending, and the regular everyday care they require."

"Who's been doing it until now?"

"Whoever I could get, wherever I could find them. I have a small crew but they can't stay onsite and make sure that the animals are well taken care of and the materials aren't stolen. I'd trust all three of these guys with my kid's safety, so I can definitely trust them with the proper care of my ranches. They'll run them as if they were their own.

"That's good to know and it must be a huge relief."

AJ's nod ended the conversation. A strained silence descended between them. Now what should he do and say? How could he get back on track? What did he really want?

Isla, thankfully, seized the reins. With a sigh, she said, "You lost your wife in death, not divorce, so your past relationship ended very differently from mine. You not only loved her deeply, but you still do. I don't begrudge you for that.

"But I have to wonder if I'm the right person for you right now. I endured a loveless marriage in which I felt like a second-class citizen for too many years. I can't risk losing myself again at that possibility. I'm living in the present for the first time in my life. I don't want to wake up next to you and say, 'Gee, we're great in bed together, but I'll never be Kate and that's the woman he truly wants.'"

"Well, that's not gonna happen. For one thing, you're nothing like her," he pointed out reasonably. Isla sniffed and gave him a cold glare. He grinned as he added, "But there is a quality you both share: no bullshit. That must be something I like."

"In her maybe. But you know what I mean. I don't think you and I are at the same place yet. And I don't have time to wait any longer. I feel like my life passed me by for decades, and now, I'm finally living and doing everything I wanted to, whether I'm alone or with someone. Life's too short for me to wait any longer, and I'm ready to live it now in my own way."

Her head tilted upwards as she studied him. His heart hammered in his chest and he stared into her deep eyes. Her close proximity intoxicated him as well as her sweet scent. She was here and available to him, which relegated his recent history to a kind of dim and hazy place in the distance. It mattered, sure, because it was a big part of him.

But in that moment with Isla right here, it was so easy for AJ to just feel good with her.

Is that what Isla meant? He honestly had no idea. This situation was unlike anything he'd ever experienced before. How could he want to be with Isla and still be in love with Kate? Was he ready to stop being sad whenever a dark mood struck him? When things happened that he least expected, should he fake it for Isla's benefit?

Isla waited, staring up at him. She naturally hoped he'd say something to ease the tension of the situation.

Sighing when he remained silent, she shook her head. "You have your solid memories. I have my life to live. I need to live right now. You had a very different marriage from mine and you believe you've already lived your best life. Mine is just getting started. See what I mean? We're not on the same page."

Why weren't they? AJ's best life happened during his years of marriage to Kate. But saying his life was virtually over didn't ring true now, although it did only a few short months ago. Before he met Isla. Her presence brightened his ordinary days and made him feel better.

He knew what she was asking of him. Isla wanted to be the first and only woman in his life. Not a placeholder or a substitute. Was he ready to give that to her today?

He doubted it. He clearly understood everything she said

and he agreed. She should live a good life from now on. Her marriage failed her. He tried to imagine how hard it would be for him to consider playing second fiddle to a dead spouse. He agreed wholeheartedly she should not.

But he didn't want her to leave him yet.

His feelings for her hadn't become more profound. The answer still eluded him. He had no heart-stopping proclamations to make or epiphanies to disclose.

All he could say now was: don't leave.

She started to pass him and his arm stopped her before he thought it out. He found her waist and wrapped his other arm around her. Leaning closer, he brought her near him. Her profile was to him, so he bent downwards until his mouth touched the top of her head. She let out a small sigh and leaned towards him. He moved closer and his warm breath touched her face. She shuddered at his barely-there presence.

The air between them was so volatile, it would have ignited if a match were lit.

His other hand found the inside of her arm just below her elbow and he gently felt the skin there, rubbing it back and forth. She froze so he leaned down and kissed the side of her face, nuzzling her hairline and moving towards her ear, he said as honestly as he could, "I can't promise you anything. I won't either. But right now, I want you and no one else."

She shuddered against him, and tried to stand up. "I refuse to endure that deep hurt again."

"I could never deliberately do anything to hurt you."

She leaned toward his mouth and he kissed her again. "I believe you. You aren't very good at this."

He pulled her closer and turned her body to face his as he kissed her mouth again. Then he smiled and said, "I beg to differ, and I think I'm quite skilled at this."

She smiled as she held his hand. "I meant dating. You'd

have to own that you are with me. Out loud to a town that still see's you as you see yourself, as *Kate's husband*. Can you really imagine publicly dating me?"

"Right. And after dancing half naked in flour with a strange man your daughter didn't know, you blushed and grew so flustered when she came in that I daresay you're not completely *there* either."

"Damn it. Fine, okay I see your point. But I'm not the victim of a tragic love story. It's too much to compete with, AJ. I can't do it. I know that now."

"Okay, I admit you're right. I can't undo my past either. But I can be here in the present with you. Let's start slow. One date. One night. And see how things work out."

"Your sincerity makes you dangerous."

"No one in the whole world considers me dangerous."

"You're dangerous to me."

He tilted his head and replied, "Maybe you are to me too."

A blush filled her entire face. "There's a lot to consider besides our feelings. Maggie is staying with me now. So there goes…"

"Your comfortable bed. Mine is no more than a board on the ground."

She eyed him with disdain. "That isn't all I meant."

He noticed the gleam in her eyes. "Right. Our big, annoying families might judge us. It's odd to watch Grandma and Grandpa share a budding romance. But it's doable. I think it is anyway. I don't want you to leave me right now. That's the only thing I know for sure."

Her mouth twisted back and forth. "Damn you. I was planning to leave. I came here already convinced I couldn't do this."

"This?"

"Play the role of substitute woman to a widower. I don't want to be relegated to that person."

He squeezed her waist and brought her closer. "I don't feel like you're a substitute. But I also can't fully say what all this is."

"I know." She eyed him more closely. Grumpy.

He chuckled at the side-eye she gave him, pulling her into his arms. His grin faded as he finally said more seriously, "What if you just stayed here tonight? We can start there."

"Where?"

"We can decide to get together whenever it works for us."

"Are there any topics we can't discuss because they're off limits?"

"No. We also agree to be brutally honest."

"Then it's a deal. Brutal honesty and starting with one night."

He released her and turned, taking her hand as he started towards the room he was currently using to sleep in. It would have to do for now. Their two daughters made that their only option. At least they had some privacy here. That seemed pretty important now. Isla didn't even pause to glance around or wrinkle her nose. She yanked off his shirt and he did the same to her. With greedy, hungry grins, they embraced before falling together on the bed.

CHAPTER 13

*L*ATER, MUCH LATER, AJ was holding Isla and he looked into her eyes. "Where do we go from here? I should have just let you walk out, but the truth is, I can't stand the thought of not seeing you. I've been miserable since our first night together at the bakery, thinking about *you,* and longing to be beside you again."

She closed her eyes because his words profoundly affected her. When her eyelids fluttered back open, she grimaced, "You know what I find so hard about dating you? The answer that first pops into my brain whenever I contemplate it?'

"What is it?"

She buried her face into the pillow, shaking her head. "I'm so ashamed that I don't even want to give it voice now."

"But we agreed so you have to. Honesty and all that…"

Peeking up, Isla let only the side of her face show. "Okay, fine. But you'll hate me for it. My first thought was be snarky and resentful about Kate, *but* I don't want to detest her or get jealous of her or feel like I'm competing with a dead woman."

"And my response is, I can only go by what happened the other night. When I'm with you, I'm not thinking about Kate. But when I'm not with you? I think about her. And none of that helped me figure out how to approach you."

"Well, you took making it awkward to a new level."

He dropped his chin, chagrinned. "Even Mack noticed you were mad at me."

"You deserved it."

"Well he was on your side. But I think that was mostly from his sugar coma caused by the drug you make but disguise as cupcakes."

She smiled and smacked her lips. "That's how you derail me. Your humor and sweetness are irresistible. But that doesn't give you any excuse for the long delay."

He gave her a squeeze and grinned. "Really? Since the new you is so full of confidence, why didn't you contact me? You want it old-fashioned in some ways but not others? Should I make all the orchestrations?"

She twisted her lips. "Damn. Maybe you've a point. And do I resent that. Fine, I guess that makes it much clearer as to what I need to do."

He nodded. "Which leads back to the endless question: how do we handle this? Both of us are admittedly out of practice."

"Only some parts of it."

He had to grin at her suggestive words. "True. Only some parts. But I have to ask what's next and when?"

"Hmmmm..." Isla shrugged. "I guess we'll find out what's next now?"

His heart raced at the way she looked at him, so hungry for love and also, so vulnerable. She wanted more but she didn't trust him. He completely understood why. His heart seemed to lodge in his throat as he said, "I want to know what's next without the input of our daughters. I want only ourselves to decide."

"Then let's start right now and see..." She reached upwards to grab his neck while he simultaneously pulled her against his body. Their mouths met and the first kiss they shared felt so wonderful and familiar.

After several long moments of clutching each other and kissing, he nuzzled her neck, saying, "We may have issues, but this isn't one of them. We're both fantastic at this."

"Fantastic is right," Isla agreed, tilting her head back. They indulged the one part of their newfound closeness that worked the best and made them the happiest.

∽

KNOCKING WOKE AJ UP. Groggily he opened his eyes and blinked a few times, but remained totally incoherent. Why was he so vacant? What day was it? Where was he?

He waited a moment for the pain to prick his heart like an ice pick in his chest. Kate. Kate was still dead and gone.

That's how he started every morning after he woke up. He was spared only a few seconds when it wasn't foremost in his thoughts, sapping his energy, attention and focus. But then reality hit him like a concrete sack being swung at his head. Kate was dead. He was alone. The years he had left to live would be without her. What could he do? How could he endure it? How did he make it through this day, or any other day, knowing Kate was dead? Why was he still here?

A sound startled him and he turned his head.

Isla.

Things weren't the same today. Isla was here with him, this morning. Curled on her side and snoring softly, she seemed to be in a deep sleep. Her hand was near his chest and her head was nestled in his shoulder. He started to relax and go back to sleep.

The knocking started again. He wasn't imagining it. Leaning down, he kissed the top of her head and paused to savor the perfect moment.

The fresh realization of his calf being scratched by Isla's toenail caused him to kiss her again and he smiled at the pain.

He was so glad she was there beside him.

Then the knocking grew more insistent. Extracting himself from the small twin bed, he scanned the room for a pair of sweats and a t-shirt. Rubbing his hand through his hair, he stumbled out of the room but was careful to shut the door tightly. Bright, blinding morning sun filled the curtain-less windows, making odd patterns all over the floor. Blinking at the brightness, he finally reached the door.

AJ was startled to find his son standing there. Of course. Sure. Why not? Naturally, Asher had to interrupt him with Isla, since it was his turn. First, it was Cami. Did they plan it in advance? Like a tag-team to thwart the old man's sex nights?

Of course, neither Asher nor Cami knew in advance because AJ didn't even know. His two children spent the last two years taking turns checking up on him daily.

But now, for the first time since Kate died, he resented their ministrations.

He wanted to wake up slowly and stay in bed with Isla. He wanted to feel her wake up next to him. He planned to make love to Isla, very slowly and deliberately. That was how he expected his morning to start. Not confronting his son first thing to tell him how healthy he was...

He appreciated his children's love and concern but maybe it was time to give him a smidgeon of credit for living well and turn to other things in their lives.

How unfair. But they had no way of knowing sex made him feel better than everything else he tried.

"Damn, Dad. Were you still sleeping? It's nine o'clock. What took you so long to answer the door?"

"I *was* sleeping." To be fair, Asher knew AJ woke at six am every single day and immediately got up. They lived together and AJ was always the first one up every morning, making a pot of coffee. The hour wasn't early for AJ. And Asher couldn't possibly have expected him to be asleep.

Asher walked past AJ straight into the house out of habit. Glancing at the closed bedroom door, AJ hoped Isla was still asleep. It was a possibility. She'd made arrangements to have Maggie open Cowboys & Cupcakes. That request hadn't been easy to ask, and Maggie had been shrill in response. But at least that meant Isla got to be there with him this morning. So he slept three hours later then he usually did.

AJ really hoped she stayed put so he could have the chance to tell Asher, at a later time, about his new involvement with her. Maybe it could happen in a calm, well-thought-out way, without any drama or awkward silences. But not today while she was in his bedroom.

"Seriously, Dad. What's up? Another rough night?" Asher's voice drew AJ's attention back to him. Yes, a truly physically exhausting night. AJ loved every minute of it and did not want to discuss it with his son.

"Something like that."

"Mom? Nightmares?"

"No. I slept like the dead. I was just very tired."

AJ wandered into the kitchen to make the coffee. He had to play it cool or Asher would start grilling him. Sometimes his kids stayed for minutes, other times for an hour or more. Hopefully, Asher had something important to do today and this visit would be a quick one.

"Your turn today, huh?" AJ asked as he scanned the cabinet for coffee filters and took the coffee can out.

"No. I actually came here to talk to you about something important." At least Asher didn't bother to beat around the bush. AJ found it sweet that his grown children cared so much.

But his words hung in the air ominously. What could be so important that Asher needed to talk about? Who could it be but Isla? Pausing, he stared across the room at his son. Did Asher know? The grave look on Asher's face suggested he was seriously disturbed or upset by it. At least he wasn't afraid to face it.

"Okay. Let me get a pot of coffee going." He finished measuring the grounds and pressed the button to start the coffee maker. When it finally stopped sputtering and became silent, AJ filled two cups with the fresh coffee and brought them to the small eating table. Asher flopped down to drink it. Blowing on his cup, he nodded and said, "Thanks. I didn't sleep much last night either."

"Why? What's going on? Is everything okay?" AJ winced, realizing he was so caught up in his own drama, he forgot to be a father to his kids. He'd grown selfish to think everything that went wrong was rooted in his loss of Kate and their concern over him. What if something happened to Daisy or Asher's business or…?

"Actually, yes. I'm just worried how to tell you this. I don't know how you'll take it."

Okay, it wasn't about Isla or gossip rumors or sex. It was about Asher. "What's going on, son?"

"It's… well, Daisy was offered a position at a well-known law firm to help with a high profile case. It's quite a pay bump and more prestigious so it's good to have on her resume, and it fits right in with her end goal."

"Being a judge?"

"Yes."

AJ leaned back and his heart dropped a little. "And that can't happen here. Not in River's End or Brewster." Daisy had her own small practice in Brewster. It was a town bigger than River's End, but not by much and few people knew where it was.

"Well? Tell me more. Where? Where is it?"

"Yakima. It's not in Seattle, so there's that. She is thinking it will take a year or so. She's hiring someone to oversee her practice in Brewster with every intention of coming back. In the short in-term, I can find a job on one of the ranches in Yakima. They surround the city and Daisy doesn't mind commuting. We agreed after we married to never separate again. So we are doing this together."

"Of course you should go and not separate. She is far more important than any place."

AJ sighed and blew on the coffee before him. Yakima wasn't impossibly inaccessible to visit, but it wasn't as close as down the street or seeing Asher every day. AJ was spoiled in having both of his kids and their families close by for most of the time. But he remembered the years when Cami was abroad on foreign soil and AJ only got to see her a few times a year. Yakima? AJ decided he could see them weekly. But still. It was a huge change. Hence Asher's hesitation in telling him.

They became close as brothers since Kate's death.

And of course, the daily check-ins. No doubt Asher had been stressed to leave those all to Cami. But in truth, he knew all of Asher's hesitation was really because he would worry about leaving AJ in his grief.

"First, tell Daisy how proud I am and happy for her."

Asher flashed a lopsided smile. "I will. I appreciate that."

"I'll miss you around here. But of course, you *have* to go. She deserves every chance and opportunity to achieve her goals. That girl is meant to accomplish wonderful things and an unusual job that most people only dream about. Her ambitions are high and that's what makes her Daisy."

"Remember when we ended it years ago and almost didn't stay together?"

"Yes, and you can do this. You can be a rancher and let her stretch her wings as a lawyer. Marriage takes patience, changes and compromise. I see you both excelling in that. Which makes me even prouder."

Asher toyed with the handle on his cup. "I'm not so noble. It helps that it's only a year or so. This one case should take that long and she believes it will be beneficial for her future. I've known about it for a few weeks. I just couldn't decide what to do about Sugar Hill Ranch. Then Mack called and told me you'd hired him, Justin and Tyrone."

AJ gave him a look, but his grin faded. "Asher, you can also sell the ranch to buy one in Yakima. Sugar Hill is yours to do with whatever you choose to do to make your life with your family work. It's not mine. Your mother and I gave you the ranch so you could start out with something. We never regretted it. Hell, I can buy it from you too."

"Dad... it's already yours."

"Let's not argue again, Asher. It's not mine. It's yours and it always has been."

Asher ducked his head. He always found it hard to accept the generous gifts AJ and Kate gave him. They didn't adopt him until he was thirteen and he was eternally grateful for that. "But we are coming back. I have no reason to sell it. I just have to take an extended break. Will you watch out for it while I'm away?"

"Of course. Don't give it a second thought. And Mack will be right there."

"Knowing you're here to oversee it makes it possible to

consider. I've worked too hard at that place to leave it with just anyone. Maybe the timing was just right."

"Mack was planning to work the ranch beside yours. Helping you out as needed. But I'm sure he'd agree to do both while you're gone. It is good timing and everything seems to be coming together, ending with Mack."

"Are you sure you're okay with this?"

Sighing and leaning back, AJ nodded. "I know you feel responsible for me, but you're not. I'm responsible for me. You have to live your best life with your family. I appreciate the concern and all you've done for me, but I can't be the only reason you stay here. That's no way to live and I won't let you."

"Cami already knows. She said—"

There was a thump.

Asher tilted his head and glanced at AJ, and then toward the bedroom, his eyebrows furrowing in visible puzzlement. "Did you get a dog?"

"No. I—" AJ blew the air out of his mouth. Here he went again, embarrassed, unsure and not willing to admit anything. It was time to stop doing that. Nodding to himself, as if the two AJs were agreement, he sat up straighter. "I had someone spend the night."

There. He said it. As diplomatically as he could, he told Asher what he'd done. Asher's face scrunched up. "Someone? Like Mack... or somebody? You guys end up drinking too late to stand up? I know he was excited about getting the biggest raise and promotion he ever got."

Crap. It didn't occur to Asher that his old man might have a little spark left inside him? "No. Not a man. A... woman. I had a woman stay over."

Incredulous and shocked, Asher's eyes met AJ's. Asher could not conceal the astonishment written all over his face. "Oh."

AJ twitched but tried to keep his expression serene and mild. Like he had women overnight all the time.

"Cami knows. Now you do too. I planned to tell you in my own time to make it less awkward. It was weird with your sister too. But since you two infiltrate so much of my life I can't hide anything from you." His lips twitched at his realization. Shaking his head, he said, "Not such a bad problem to have, I've decided."

Asher's face was pale. He was having a physical reaction to the news. AJ wasn't being overly sensitive or imagining it.

"You're seeing someone now?"

Was he? What should he say? How could he define what was happening with Isla? He met a great sex partner that made him feel connected, alive and better than he had since Kate died. But that wasn't all she was. If he just needed sex, he could have gotten it with anyone. He was completely fascinated by Isla.

"Seeing someone? Yes. It's so new, it's hard to explain and I know it's weird since she's not your mother and all that."

Tilting his head, Asher nodded. "I guess you have to move on too. You can't just stay here forever living all alone. I just…"

"Never thought you'd have to witness it?"

"Maybe." Asher's gaze drifted away. "But fate or karma or the universe didn't ask me what I wanted when it made Mom so sick she died." Bitterness laced his tone.

"Fate or karma or the universe brought you to us. Sometimes, what you don't ask for or expect turns out to be something good."

Asher leaned back in his seat and slouched as he sighed. "That sounds hopeful. I haven't heard you sound so optimistic since Mom died."

"Because I wasn't."

"So tell me... who is she?" Asher shuddered. "Never thought I'd be asking my old man that."

"No, but there's a first in all things, huh? She's Isla." There was only one Isla in town.

"The cupcake lady?" His expression widened in surprise before he shook his head. "Duh. Of course she is. She's very attractive and the only new person to show up this year. So... it makes sense. How long?"

"Not long at all. We were friends."

"And now it's become more than friends?"

"Looks that way."

Asher nodded towards the bedroom. "So that's who I heard. And the reason why you weren't up at nine am."

"Yes."

"Okay. I think I'll take my leave now. I said what I came to say. I'm glad we discussed those things and got it out there. But I just a need a few moments to process it."

"Are you going home to get angry?"

Standing up, Asher's expression melted. "No. Dad. If you can enjoy a friend's company and you're happy, I'm glad to hear it."

"Me too. I didn't know I was looking for anyone. But so far, I'm glad I met Isla." She was fun too. And seeing her was something he always looked forward to. He finally had something and someone to share his hope with.

He walked Asher to the door, and Asher gave him a hug before leaving that almost made AJ cry. That went better then he expected. Lacking the time to practice or prepare himself, it went amazingly well.

As soon as the front door closed, Isla opened the bedroom door.

"Did he hear me? I'm sorry. I got out of bed before I heard your voices and tried to remain quiet."

"He heard you."

"Oh." Her face flushed as she stepped back and flopped into a chair. "I hope he's not mad."

Seeing her worry, AJ walked over and knelt before her. Taking her hand in his, he kissed it and replied, "I told him that I've started seeing you. I said I was sorry if it was hard to hear, but I wasn't sorry you were here with me. Or something close to that."

Her eyes widened, along with her mouth. "How did he take it?"

"Fine, surprisingly. I felt odd and weird but he said he was glad I met someone who makes me feel better."

Isla lifted her other hand and cupped his cheek. Her gaze on him was long and deep. "And have you met someone who makes you feel better?"

He nodded, holding her stare. "I have."

Her mouth twisted and she said, "You're getting better at this."

"Are you saying my skills extend outside of the bed?"

"Yeah."

Leaning back on his heels, he shook his head.

"What is it?" she asked softly.

"I thought it would be more dramatic."

"What would be more dramatic? Explaining your sex life to your adult children? Or having a woman in your life that isn't Kate?"

"Option two. I don't know what I pictured. But I guess I thought there'd be some huge moment where I'd just *know* it was okay to move on. Or... or I don't know exactly. Some kind of sign from her. But... There is no such a thing. I just have to decide. For myself."

"No. There is no such thing. You have to decide. I can't help you there."

"I'm making the choice because I'm ready now but only because it's you. I don't care where this might lead anymore.

I like how it started and I like having you here right now. Isn't that enough?"

Her smile was bright and warm. "It depends. It could be. Will you call yourself my boyfriend?"

He tilted his head and sucked in a breath of air. That was a new label. He hadn't worn it in more than three decades. But it was a heck of a lot better than widower. He really liked Isla so he'd don the new label if only for her sake.

"Yes."

"Then it's enough."

"What will your daughter say about this?"

She smirked and leaned forward to kiss his lips. "Are you afraid of what she'll say?"

"Truthfully, yes. A little apprehensive."

"She'll be okay eventually. Her husband betrayed her and she just had her third child. I know what that's like. It's a different kind of death, but just as filled with grief."

"Is she staying with you indefinitely?"

She tilted her head. "Perhaps. Have I said too much? Life is full of drama, and the fights and conflicts never stop. I don't expect you to deal with mine or start attending all of our family activities. But someday, I might ask you to do that. With me. As a couple. Are you open to doing that someday if all goes well?"

He blew some air into his cheeks. "Yes. Someday. When it feels right for everyone involved."

Her smile was quick at his delicate wording. "You mean Maggie?"

He nodded. "Mostly. I mean Maggie. But I also don't know the rest of your kids. So… all of it."

She kissed him and AJ added, "Now that Maggie and her family need to live somewhere… I might have a short term solution. I've recently come into possession of an impressive rental property; it's called Sugar Hill Ranch."

Isla's eyes widened. "Asher and Daisy's ranch?"

"They're moving for about a year. Daisy got a job offer in Yakima she can't refuse. I just hired Mack Baker to live on the property as foreman. But the house is huge. I don't want strangers there, to tell you the truth. But your daughter? Although I don't know her, I trust you."

Isla peered at him incredulously. "AJ Reed, I sense an ulterior motive. Did you make this offer so you could resume having sex in my bed?"

He grinned and his smile was contagious. "I sure did. My back still hurts from that piece of crap bed I sleep on and yours felt better than a cloud."

"Buying a new bed would be a lot easier and much cheaper."

"No… I like your bed, and your place." He gestured to the rundown room they were sitting in. "This is not my home. I was in a holding pattern."

Her gaze wavered. "AJ, I'm not ready to move in together…"

AJ began laughing before he kissed her mouth. "Neither am I. But I'd like to spend more time at your place. Not necessarily at mine."

Her cheeks burned brightly with a blush and she finally just said, "Oh."

He held her face in his hand. "Yeah, oh. Why don't you think about it? Maggie could have some space to think and heal and do whatever she needs to do. Mack is onsite in case of any emergencies, so she wouldn't be alone. And I go out there several times a week to oversee the work on it anyway…"

Her mouth met his in a long kiss. "It sounds full of promise…"

He held her gaze and read the meaning in her eyes. He

was sure she understood him. "It does, doesn't it? *So* full of promise?"

She savored his last sentence. He waited for a long time before he added, "Isla? You don't know it yet, but I always keep my promises."

Her smile was so brilliant it could have blinded him. "I can't wait to find that out…"

CHAPTER 14

~ *Cami* ~

"IT'S WEIRD, HUH?" CAMI said to Asher. Her gaze was pinned on her father as he held Isla's hand to guide her down the steps of the three-story house that made up the main dwelling at Sugar Hill Ranch.

Asher didn't need any clarification to know what she meant. "Yes."

"But it's so good to see him smile again. For real. I never imagined he'd find the strength to move on from Mom." She stared down at her hands and added, "As juvenile as that sounds."

"It's just what it is, Cams. We lost our mom. He lost a wife. We both know what their relationship was. I find some comfort in that."

"That's why he was so devastated. It was impossible for me to enjoy an entire day while thinking of him stuck in one of those stupid ranches, all alone, in the darkness of his heart and thoughts. This is honestly easier because I know there's a good chance he's doing okay now. But it's also harder in other ways. Which, I know, sounds selfish."

Asher shook his head. "No, you sound like a daughter who lost her mother."

She cleared her throat and said, "I always pictured a big, momentous epiphany when Dad would explain how he could move on from mom. I thought there would be some kind of… sign. But now I'm realizing it just kind of happened one day. I childishly almost expected him to come to me or you to get permission…"

"I think he might have had an epiphany, but being Dad, he would never vocalize it."

"You're right. Did he ask you to bring Isla today?"

Asher shrugged. "No. I asked him to bring her. I'm leaving soon and I wanted to know her as more than just the cupcake woman. You know?"

"Yeah, we should since our visits might soon include her."

"Might."

Cami shook her head and dabbed her tears again. "I can't believe you won't be living here anymore."

"For a year. Not forever. You and Charlie missed half my youth. I'm a few hours away by car, not a plane ticket."

"Good point. But now I live here. I lost my mom, and now that my father is dating again, I want my brother close by."

"I would have stayed in a heartbeat. But Daisy…"

"Is an amazing, ambitious person to whom you are drawn because of that and other things. You're always willing to support and follow her because that's who she is. Yeah, I get that." She was also referring to her very ambitious husband, Charlie Rydell, with whom she traveled half the planet.

Asher chuckled. "We married the same people, huh?"

"They're cousins after all."

"We'll stay in touch, right? We won't fall to the wayside. It took us years to bridge the gap when we didn't know each other. But we both lost our mom."

"I promise to stay in touch."

They became quiet. Asher nodded to her teenage boys, now eighteen, as they helped him lift the heavy dresser while Daisy guided them. They were invited to participate not only for their youth, but also their strong muscles and endurance today. "How did they take Grandpa having a girlfriend?"

She let out a big laugh. That was the only amusing thing about it. "Isaac pretended to fall to the floor at the grossness of it and Ethan was 'blinded by the images' I described, or so he said. They then got up and laughed their heads off. They're both fine with it, but they find it difficult to think about Grandpa like that. Ethan asked if they should call her *Granny* and I said no, guessing she'd be insulted if he did. So I guess all the trauma I expected was unfounded."

Asher laughed at her description. "Ethan asked Dad about working for him when he graduates. You okay if he ends up being a rancher?"

"He won't ask me for my advice. I'm okay as long as he has a strong work ethic. So, yes. Besides, all my favorite men are ranchers."

Asher ducked his head as if to say, *Ahh, shucks.* "Who? Dad and me? Your husband is the polar opposite."

"I have twin boys. There's always hope..." She grinned and shook her head. "Really, I don't care. They will be whomever they are and do what works for them, and that's all that matters to me. I'm just here to support them until they find their own way."

Asher fist-bumped her.

"The only complaint I have is Dad renting my place to her..." Asher nodded to indicate the woman off to the side.

Maggie Whitlock. She had a married name but she wasn't using it anymore. She went back to her maiden name. There was an entire story right there. But Cami wasn't interested in it. She tolerated her dad's new girlfriend, but hell if she would suddenly become a new step-sister.

"Yeah. Dad isn't particularly fond of her. Claims you have to wear ear plugs when she starts shrieking."

"Then why did he give her such an awesome place to stay?"

"It's only temporary until she figures out her shit. And why do you think? To get her out of the place where he spends half his time." Asher shuddered. "Ugh. I feel like Ethan and Isaac at the thought of what you just said. But I'm also glad he's not alone."

"He owns an entire network of ranches in Reed Ranch Enterprises and he has a girlfriend. Dad's okay, Asher. For real. You can leave River's End and know he's really okay. It's hard, but it's a good thing too. Life moves on. Mom told me that. I just never thought Dad would do it. But he really has."

"True. I guess we all have to move on now, huh? Your boys are almost grown and you'll be empty-nesters soon."

"With plans to start traveling again."

He smiled. "That doesn't shock me."

"And you and Daisy have new mountains to climb."

"I think we might look into fostering a child with the possibility of adoption. I should clarify that, fostering a youth in their teens."

Cami's heart swelled with joy. "Just like Mom and Dad did?"

"Exactly like Mom and Dad did with us." Asher turned his gaze towards his dad. "As hard as it's been for the last few years, I would never change what happened because it's the reason we became the people we are now."

"I see so much karmic symmetry if you end up adopting a foster youth."

"Or two." Asher grinned, pinning his gaze on the blond head of his wife. Daisy happened to catch him staring and she gave him a little wave and a long look. Cami admired the special look they shared.

"Mom would be, no Mom *is* so proud of you."

"I learned from the best." He turned his gaze to AJ.

Cami did too and tears filled her eyes. But something new was on her face: a sappy smile beneath the tears. AJ was the best in everything. The best dad and grandpa and his and Kate's love and marriage were the most valuable gifts that guided her entire life.

"We were lucky to have the real thing," she whispered.

"Luckier still, to have him now."

"Yes," she agreed.

AJ glanced up and found them both staring at him. He looked at Cami and conveyed a silent message, asking if he should come over there? Cami shook her head no, then she smiled and gave him a little wave. AJ smiled back and nodded. Despite this emotional day, Cami was okay.

Asher and Daisy were relocating and her father had already begun moving on. Her two boys were nearly adults, and she didn't fail to notice any of that.

But she was okay with it.

"Cami? Asher? Feel like getting some cupcakes at the shop? The truck's loaded but we thought we deserved a treat after all this heavy lifting." Daisy called out, breaking her reverie.

Cami blinked and nodded. Then she smiled at her brother as she got up to go to the shop of her father's girlfriend. *First time for everything*, she thought. When Sugar Hill Ranch was in her rearview mirror, Cami thought, *there's a last time for everything too.*

Such was life. Nothing was ever finished or done, no matter how it seemed. That's what made it so damn hard… and so damn beautiful.

EPILOGUE

~TWO YEARS LATER~

"I'm here, Dad. What's up?"

Asher had been back in the Rydell River Valley after his and Daisy's fourteen month hiatus. Once more, Asher was part of the every day life of AJ.

And Isla.

For now they were mostly inseparable. In fact that was part of what he had to say to Asher.

They met for cupcakes, of course. Sipping the coffee, he glanced at his son. "I have a few things to say and if you can't or don't want to do any, or all of it, be honest. Okay?"

"Sounds serious." He frowned.

"First, everything is fine health wise and all. This is more about future stuff."

Asher blew on the coffee before him, he waited a beat and said quietly, "There was a time when you didn't foresee a decent future."

"I didn't. No. But then I met Isla."

"I'm glad you met Isla then." AJ's heart flipped. That was hard for Asher to admit. He'd had a harder time with AJ's relationship only because he missed his mother so much.

Asher continued, "But that's not what this is about. What's going on?"

"I want to ask you to take over Reed Ranch Enterprises." AJ led with the easier news.

Startled, Asher choked on the gulp of hot coffee he'd just taken. "What? Dad! That's yours."

"No. I started it. I want you to continue it. It needs a Reed at the helm. And that son, is you."

"Where are you going?"

"I'm... retiring." He said it softly, breathing in as he said it. A deep contentment came with the words.

"Retiring? Again? Look how well that went the first time." Asher's tone grew grumpy.

He sighed. "It's time, Asher. I'm old. I need... no I want to do this. I want to putter with animals, not run what's become a bit of a local empire. I mean we are kind of land baron's now." His chest might have puffed up at that statement. For though it might have been on accident, he had done just that.

He'd created his own Reed legacy with multiple, profitable locations. He'd made it a bit of a thing in the valley. Their name. Their ranches. Far different than the Rydell River Ranch. Theirs, the Reeds, were many locations and working ranches that put out a solid output of cattle and ran an impressive bit of horses as well.

They were the grit to Jack Rydell's pretty ranch and *resort*.

It had become the best way to goad his brother-in-law. Jack would grind his teeth as AJ teased of his beloved Rydell River Ranch being more of a resort than past decades when it was only a ranch. For Jack had never wanted all the resort stuff and fanfare that had become the Rydell River Ranch's many offshoots.

"Dad. I don't know what to say. I mean I'm also a rancher. I'm not sure I even know where to start with all that."

"Your wife is a brilliant lawyer and most likely could run

circles around us both for the business end. But what do you think I knew about all this? Nothing. Nada. So if I can do it, I can train you two."

"What about Cami?"

"Well she isn't a Reed any longer. It needs a Reed."

"Dad!"

He grinned. "I'm kidding. The thing is Jack and I agreed Charlie gets a part of the Rydell River Ranch through him. So Cami is included with that. But our grandsons? They should get the Reed branch of their family. Jack has more grandkids. I don't… yet." He gave Asher a significant look. Asher rolled his eyes. "So… yeah, that's what we decided."

"You and Jack decided who gets what ranch legacy?"

He laughed with a carefree humor he'd rarely felt in his life. "Okay, and the fact that Cami already said no to my offer to split it between you and her. She has enough to do. And so Jack I had a long talk. I've created a successful business with the Reed name on it. Enough to almost rival the Rydell Legacy."

Asher leaned back, arms folded. "First, it's awesome you and Uncle Jack are hanging out again. Awful you goad him about his successful businesses. And I never knew you wanted to create a legacy."

"Neither did I. Goes to shows you, you really are never done if you're still breathing. And yeah, Jack and I are good. It was never him. I just struggled to be on the Rydell River Ranch land, our old home, and I kind of lost track of him for a time, like I did many things."

"You really trust me to take this thing over?"

"I trust you. I trust Daisy. Think of your nephews. The place you could help create for them, if they wanted it."

"And maybe my own. Daisy and I started the process to become foster parents."

AJ's heart thumped. Kate. Sometimes the little moments

snuck up and still struck him. Ah, how Kate would have loved to be here for this exact moment. To see Asher's shy, but proud smile. To realize that what they had done for Asher, had made him want to pass that chance on to some other youth. More than all the job success or fancy titles of ranches and legacy, she'd have loved to experience Asher and Daisy as parents. But not just usual parents, parents like he had Kate had been. They'd started with teenagers. Something that most didn't do. But look at what fine children they had nurtured and the wonderful human beings they had become.

He blinked rapidly to hold back the brief spark of tears. "You know how proud she'd be."

"I do."

"I am too." He added softly.

"Okay, so you want me to become THE Reed of Reed Ranch Enterprises. Anything else?"

"And... perhaps if you were comfortable with it... my best man."

Asher's mouth popped open. Then shut.

AJ rushed on. "If it's too much to ask, I get that. I just wanted you to know it would be you. First and always. But Jack will do it. Or Charlie. But I'd always first choose you."

"She agreed to marry you?"

He nodded.

Isla Whitlock had no interest in being a wife. He had no interest in making anyone his wife again.

For a good solid year and seven months that they dated they had fully agreed on that.

And then... at some point, it started to sound not so scary or strange to think about Isla as his wife.

It became not that Kate wasn't his wife, but that maybe he could have another, different wife too.

Like Isla. She'd resisted at first.

He'd kind of resisted at first, too. But the longer they talked it over, the better it sounded.

"Yes. Nothing big. Just her kids and you guys. If you're comfortable."

"Isla Reed?"

"Yes."

Asher flinched. "Are you happy?"

"Yes. I am. I want to retire with her. She does not. She wants to make cupcakes but do it part time. Her daughter will become partner with her. I'd still be around to help you, and putter here and there. But no more full days. Just… being. Enjoying. Relaxing."

It was odd to see all the old timers, truly all slowing down and becoming on the back burners. The putterers.

Long past when most did.

He was now there. But this time? He was relieved. Excited. Perhaps ready for the final act of his life.

For however long it lasted, he would live each day to his fullest. With Isla. Their joined families. Their love.

Memories still part of him, and them. But no longer quite so daily.

"Dad?" Asher said quietly. "I'd be *honored* to be your best man. To run the legacy you created, and to be THE Reed of Reed Ranches."

His heart bumped hard. He had not believed his life could move forward after Kate died. He had thought his dreams over, ambitions killed, and all joy leached forever from his future. Turns out, that was true for a long while. But then some of it morphed and changed. Things grew and others wilted. But nothing remained the same.

Time moved on. Always had. Always would. That was why life was so precious. That was why he now said the big things out loud. Thoughts. Feelings. All the words he used to not say, he now tried to share.

To his kids and grandkids, and most of all, to Isla.

Later, when Asher left with an emotional hug to him, he slipped upstairs where he lived with Isla. Who would guess Rancher AJ Reed of Reed Ranch Enterprises, would end up living in an apartment, in town, in River's End, over a cupcake shop? Odder still? He truly enjoyed it.

But emotional and tired after the meeting with Asher, and letting go of the business he never wanted, but had grown to feel proud of, he also was relieved he could soon marry the person who made all of it better.

It was only moments before Isla came in after him.

"How did it go?"

He loved she came up and asked. That she wanted to know. That he had a best friend, companion and lover in this beautiful second chance at having a wife, when he should have been long past retiring and second chances.

Reed Ranches. Isla. His kids. Grandkids. Her kids and grandkids. And perhaps as Asher just told him today, it was still going to be growing on his own side of the family.

Yes, he'd gotten a pretty amazing second chance.

He told her. He told her it all. As he always did.

Isla slipped her arms around him and sat on his lap. "I'm glad he didn't hate the idea of me becoming a Reed."

He smiled and kissed her. Looking into her eyes he teased, "I don't hate the idea either."

She let out a loud, full laugh. So warm, alive, there, with him.

Isla Reed. His wife. It sounded... right.

And still his legacy grew. Still breathing it turned out, often led to some pretty epic things.

ABOUT THE AUTHOR

Leanne Davis has a business degree from Western Washington University. She worked for several years in the construction management field before turning full time to writing. She lives in the Seattle area with her husband and two children. When she isn't writing, she and her family enjoy camping trips to destinations all across Washington State, many of which become the settings for her novels.

Made in the USA
Coppell, TX
26 April 2023